watcher

of

worlds

Whispering Woods #3

Brinda Berry

Published By Sweet Biscuit Publishing LLC
Edited by Nancy Cassidy
Cover Design by Najla Qamber Designs

Watcher of Worlds
All Rights Are Reserved. Copyright 2013 by Brinda Berry
First electronic publication: December 2013 by Etopia Press
Second electronic publication: June 2014 by Sweet Biscuit Publishing LLC

First print publication: October 2014

Digital ISBN: 978-0-9916320-4-6

Print ISBN: 978-0692316337

About the Author

Brinda Berry lives in the South with her family and two spunky cairn terriers. She's terribly fond of chocolate, coffee, and books that take her away from reality. She doesn't mind being called a geek or "crazy dog lady." When she's not working the day job or writing a novel, she's guilty of surfing the internet for no good reason.

Social media at

http://www.brindaberry.com
https://www.facebook.com/BrindaBerryAuthor
https://twitter.com/#!/Brinda_Berry

For release news, subscribe at

http://www.brindaberry.com/mailing-list.html

Acknowledgements

I'd be lost without my special people. As always, thanks to Audrey Estes for reading, supporting, promoting, and laughing. Thanks to Kristi Cheatham and Monieca West for being beyond-awesome beta readers and friends. Every writer needs critiquers as brutally honest as mine: Abbie Roads, Christina Delay, Jenn Windrow, Natalya Whitaker and Jennifer Savalli. Special shoutout to talented critique partner Kelly Crawley for reading and critiquing every single page.

You ladies rock.

Dedication

To Brent who doesn't read my books (too much kissing on the page) but supports me in everything I do. Thanks for saying I never have to sell cookware.

Chapter One

Imperfect

In a perfect world, I'd have three things: a lifetime supply of Skittles, a part-time job that didn't include extra-terrestrials, and an unbroken heart.

But I never expected perfect. I *did* wish for life closer to normal.

I crossed my arms and listened to my friend Arizona. He could charm me into anything and today he wanted me to accompany him to the woods. He'd come alone and that had been a good move. There were things I could handle and things I couldn't. I *could* handle Arizona's current modus operandi: train, capture, and train.

I *couldn't* handle facing our team leader, Regulus. The guy had owned my heart once. Then, he'd returned it—fractured in a zillion pieces of bittersweet memories.

"I've made a decision," I said. "I think you need to replace me. I don't plan on leaving you guys without an option. If my brother and I were born with synesthesia, that's two of us in Whispering Woods. Two from the same family. High percentage. There has to be more. Statistically, I'm positive that there are more people who have it. I'll find someone else who can be your portal gatekeeper."

He cocked his head to one side, presenting me with his sad-puppy face.

"Oh, come on." I resisted the urge to add 'pretty please.' Begging was not my style.

Arizona had the audacity to give me his heart-melting grin. "Now Mia. You can't be replaced. It's rare to find a synesthete who can sense portals." He reached over and placed an arm around my shoulder. "You're special." He crushed me in a side hug.

By special, he had to mean that I didn't have a backbone and could be coerced into this life that had gone from passably comfortable, to life-as-an-extreme-sport.

"Stop with the hugging. I'll go." We stood on the front porch. Winter hadn't made up its mind if it wanted to let fall hang around, or not. My hoodie would be a little warm for Arizona's favorite class, Torture Mia 101. "I need to put on a T-shirt. I'll be back in a minute."

Inside, I grumbled as I went up the stairs to my room. I understood the whole "Slips can be dangerous" and "This is serious business" and "You are more than a dowsing rod for portals" mentality that Arizona kept throwing at me. But I just wanted it to stop. Teens were supposed to say no to drugs. Why couldn't I just say no to him?

Wait a minute. I *had* said no.

The problem was that Arizona knew the main reason that I wanted—no needed—to quit. I couldn't see my ex without my chest squeezing so hard it threatened to implode. He and Regulus worked for the Interdimensional Immigration Authorities—IIA for short. I always shortened the ridiculously self-important name. The IIA had been recruiting me for months.

I changed into a T-shirt, added sneakers, and pulled my long hair into a ponytail. It wouldn't hurt to practice with Arizona one more time. Maybe I could come up with a plan to find a replacement for me. How hard could it be?

I was a little cheered by the thought and had a pep in my step. I walked outside to see him patiently waiting on the porch swing.

"'Resistance is futile.'" Arizona read the slogan on my shirt with wide smile.

I looked down at my chest and frowned. There went my good mood. "Let's get this over with."

We walked to the area where the portal had taken up residence. The portals in Whispering Woods changed according to moon phases and I had the lucky job of locating where the next one would appear. The identification of a portal had gotten exponentially easier. It pulled at me. Breaking up with Regulus must have helped me to focus my senses on things other than him.

My skin always tingled within a hundred-foot radius of the portal. Not enough to make me break a sweat, but enough to make me feel uneasy. Fifty feet away, I'd taste fizzy cola, the vibrations of the portal seeping into my mouth. Ten feet away, I'd see the shimmer of the envelope around the portal. A beautiful wave of compressed air dressing the portal's opening.

In different circumstances, it would have been inspirational, vast, or mysterious, like looking into the Grand Canyon with binoculars but with a more powerful lens.

I might even miss this. I sighed and hoped Arizona hadn't heard it. Portal detection was like scoring extra life points in my favorite video game—easy if you knew the key.

"You ready?" he asked.

"Oh yeah. Favorite part of every Saturday." My droll tone dripped with sarcasm.

"It can't be that bad to spend a few hours with me."

I looked up in surprise. "No. You know I was kidding."

His eyebrows raised a half inch.

"I'm happy to be outside and this is fine." It had been more than fine during the pre-breakup months when both Regulus and Arizona had trained with me on the weekends.

"Fine," he mocked, then found his persuasive smile again. "I want you to train near the portal. Your sensory signals should never interfere with apprehending an intruder."

"Gotcha."

"Take this bow. We need to expand from a knife. A knife only works when your target is near. Today, it's stump shooting."

I took it from his hands. "Like this?"

He nudged one of my feet. "Shoulder width apart. Stand sideways and straddle this invisible line." He scrubbed one heel across the ground. "Put your hands here and here. Most of your weight is on your back foot."

"What's Regulus doing today?" As soon as the words were out of my mouth, I wanted to take them back. It was none of my business how he spent his time. It was also a stupid thing to say since I'd refused to train with him.

I held the bow with my left hand and pulled the string. The arrow flew in a wild arc into the brush.

"I didn't tell you to release it." Arizona grimaced. "He has a paper due. Working on it with this girl from Western Civ class. Allison, I think."

My heart raced and my vision closed in at the edges.

He glanced at my face. "I'll find the arrow. It's OK."

He'd only said a paper. Not a date. A person could have a friend or a study partner and it didn't have to mean anything. And it wasn't supposed to matter if it *was* more than working on a class project. So why did it still hurt?

Whoosh.

Something massive moved in my peripheral vision. I gasped as a beast stormed through the portal at my right. The animal surged toward me. Shock froze me like a car stranded across railroad tracks. Arizona yelled at me to back up.

The panicked sounds of the horse rang through my ears. I crouched on the ground and covered my head.

"Move back," yelled Arizona.

I wanted to listen and do as he said, but I was frozen. And then an impact smacked me to the ground—the air knocked from my lungs, an elbow jammed in my side, a scream sounded in my ear. I pushed to my knees and crawled at a pace like swimming through pudding.

The woman at my side lay limp with her head lolling to one side. I moved closer and touched her arm. Her horse whinnied and kicked his hooves in the air.

Arizona moved in. "I've got her." He placed his stunner against her wrist and inserted a microchip into the flesh.

"Is she OK?" My lips quivered and nausea crept forward. "She's bleeding." I moved her hair from her face. On examination, I could tell that she was close to my age—only a teen. I stared at her model-perfect features marred by the blood.

"She's breathing," he said.

"Arizona. She's hurt."

"It's a little blood. She'll be OK."

"You can't—"

Arizona picked her up. The horse had settled and moved closer to his owner. "This won't take long, but you should go back home." He hefted the girl's body across the animal and jumped on the horse's back.

"What if she's a runaway or something?" The girl moaned as if she'd heard me.

"She doesn't have authorization to be here. She's a Slip. It doesn't matter why."

"But—"

The girl began to wiggle, trying to slip from the horse's back. Arizona fought to keep his balance.

"Where is Regulus when I need him? Hooking up with some girl," he muttered.

I sucked in a breath.

He frowned. "I didn't mean anything by that."

I knew he expected me to say—*Oh, it's OK. No big deal.*

But my lips couldn't form words because something in the denial section of my brain clicked. Total clarity in that one phrase—'hooking up with some girl.'

Before, Regulus had always followed the rules of engagement. Cardinal rule said there could be no dating in an agent's assigned area. And then we'd *happened*. We hadn't planned to fall for each other. It was like getting wet in a thunderstorm. Unavoidable. Intense. A force of nature.

The IIA had inflicted their punishment and performed a memory cleanse.

Was Regulus breaking the rules for someone else? Bile rose in my throat and I closed my eyes. Arizona thought I could go back to being friends with Regulus. He thought I could talk about Regulus dating other girls. He had no idea.

"Go home, Mia. Don't stay out here alone," he yelled over his shoulder.

I blinked back tears as he disappeared. Realization blasted me. He didn't know I was in love with Regulus. That my feelings hadn't changed. And what would the IIA plan for me if they knew? If people regularly had moments of clarity like this, they'd solve world hunger and find a cure for cancer. Or quit persecuting innocent girls like the unauthorized dimension traveler in Arizona's grip.

Quit making bad life choices.

I knew what I needed to do. If I were smart, I'd walk away from the friend zone and never look back.

Chapter Two

Jingle Bells

I detested planned surprises.

I could read the expectation in the air from the shimmery orange vibe that glowed like a Cheetos binge gone bad.

A few months ago, my friends had discovered my secret. The secret I'd hidden so teachers and doctors wouldn't treat me like an amped up sensory perception freak. So friends wouldn't ask.

Synesthesia. The condition sounded like the name of an electronic punk band. I'd made the full round of emotions about my sensory perception and being able to find portals. First, I'd hid it like you hide an ugly rash. Later, I'd learned to trust my friends with my secret. I'd even embraced it.

Now, I was back to wishing for normal.

Working with Regulus and Arizona was like playing Pop Goes the Weasel—a surprise around every corner. And did I mention I hate surprises?

Give me predictable any day. Then I could be ready. It's why I made sure I knew the contents of every box under the Christmas tree.

I tore the green foil paper from the side of the gift box and I forced that wow-you-didn't, happy look on my face. Dad had bought a new gaming system for me.

"Oh, Dad. You shouldn't have. Really. It's too much."

He arched a single brow. "You don't like it." His suspicious tone accused me.

I rose from the sofa and walked over to his recliner. I did the jazz hands and added more enthusiasm to my voice. "No. I love, love, love it." It was the peppy, exaggerated enthusiasm I reserved only for him and my best friends. "See?" I gave him a bear hug.

"I didn't know what to get you and I thought you might be tired of Pete's hand-me-down gaming systems." He still wore the tight smile that came with talking about my older brother who'd left home and never returned. The son that he might never see again.

This Christmas, the mention of Pete didn't make my stomach clench and feel like it held a thick doughy knot deep in the center. I knew my missing brother was alive even if my dad didn't. My dad's pained expression prompted me to try harder and smile bigger. He couldn't know the truth. It was too dangerous.

"Well, you know me and it's about time I had a PlayStation that wasn't for sale in the Dark Ages.

You've mastered Christmas shopping." I plopped onto the couch.

A gaming system definitely beat last year's presents—a Christmas sweater, old lady perfume, and teen girl self-help books. Those gifts had gone to the closet netherworld.

"What did Emily get for Christmas?" he asked, nonchalance oozing from his words. He pretended to study the collector edition comics I had given him.

I could see the wheels turning in his mind. He was using Emily's presents as a gauge for how well he'd done. Ridiculous. Emily and I were as different as people could get except for the fact that we got each other. Really, truly understood one another.

"The usual. Clothes and more clothes." I wrinkled my nose to punctuate my feelings about gifts my best friend had received. "Chi iron, new car stereo-"

"Her new car didn't come with a stereo?"

"Not good enough. She wants stuff that I don't care about. You know that."

"I don't know who would give their kid an iron." Dad gave a snort and lifted his head a little higher.

I stared at him for a moment, not comprehending. "Chi iron," I said, holding back a grin that threatened to bubble out. "For straightening hair."

"Oh." His chin dropped.

We sat looking at the boxes scattered across the coffee table that encompassed the entirety of our celebration. I thanked goodness Christmas was almost over. It hadn't been like this when Pete lived at home.

My cairn terrier, Biscuit, gave a little shake of his wheat-colored head and tugged at the paper strewn across the living room floor.

Dad checked his phone. After a moment he thumbed through a magazine on the end table before giving up and tossing it aside. "Why don't you ask some friends over to play some of these video games? I'll hook you up to the television while you call."

I gnawed the corner of my thumbnail. "Nah. Really, Dad. That's not necessary."

"I haven't seen Emily since break started."

"She can't come. She's on grandparent overload. Christmas at their house is a nightmare of Peggy Sue orchestrated festivities." I rolled my eyes. Em's mom was a bundle of frenzied holiday energy.

"What about Austin?" Dad got out of the recliner and grabbed the box I had opened. He extracted a small knife from his pocket and cut the seal. "He hasn't been here either."

"Yeah," I said. "I'm not really talking with him much these days.

"Jan?"

I raised one eyebrow to let him know what I thought of that ludicrous idea. "Haven't hung out with her since junior high." He'd be naming my grade school friends soon if I didn't stop him. "Everybody is really busy during the holidays."

"You're not talking with Regulus either?"

"Not so much since the breaking up thing." Five seconds passed and all the muscles in my throat tightened. I inhaled and exhaled slowly, not wanting him to sense me doing it.

Dad nodded solemnly and examined his present. Without looking up, he said, "Regulus and Arizona could both come over. You were friends with Regulus before you dated him, right?"

I didn't answer. I leaned my head back on the couch to study the blades of the ceiling fan.

"You could do things with him that friends do. Like video games."

Terrific. Dad thought he needed to give me relationship advice.

"Dad, I don't need company. I'm fine." I grabbed the nearest scrap of wrapping paper and stuffed it into the trash bag. The candy box beckoned to me, so I leaned over and popped a chocolate-covered cherry in my mouth. Speaking through the gooey confection, I muttered, "You're smothering me."

"I've tried to be it all for you, and I know that I'm not good at mothering." He stared at the inside of the opened box like it might hold some instruction booklet on how to handle a seventeen-year-old.

"I said smothering," I enunciated after unsticking pink cherry filling from my tongue. "OK. Just stop. This is Christmas. I have the best dad in the world who is about to hook up my freaking awesome new PlayStation."

I stuck my hands inside the cardboard box to pull out the cables. Looking at my dad's solemn expression, he was thinking about Pete. A faraway look in his eye made me swallow, blink, and count to ten. I wanted to tell my dad what I knew. That Pete was OK. But I couldn't. If I did, I'd be the little sister who couldn't keep her mouth shut.

I couldn't stand another minute of the dreary mood. Crying on Christmas was a crime I wouldn't commit. "I'm calling somebody. Several somebodies. It'll be a party." Taking a deep breath, I looked around until I spotted my cell phone.

My thumbs danced over the buttons.

"Hey All. Christmas party at my house. Loud music. Pizza and more sugar than you can process. Slightly somber dad. Extra peppy hostess."

I prayed my friends would come and lift my house from its current state of gloom.

An hour later, Dad stood in the kitchen making homemade pizza with store-bought crust and my favorite ingredients. He shimmied around the kitchen island in time to the beat of an Aerosmith song from his 80s station. I sat on a bar stool at the end, nibbling on slices of pepperoni and playing a game on my phone.

The doorbell rang. I leaped off the barstool and hurtled for the door, desperate to relieve the boredom. I flung open the door, not really surprised that the person in front of me would be able to show up at the last minute on Christmas Eve night. The wind blew the door open wide and I hugged my arms around my body.

My ex-boyfriend Regulus stood staring me.

His dark hair curled along the edge of his cream wool turtleneck and a shy smile teased one corner of his mouth. He held a brown box tucked under his arm and had one hand shoved into his jeans pocket.

I knew I was only a synesthete and couldn't make time stop, but I'd swear the clock hands stood still. In the moment we stood silent, a boa constrictor of jealousy wrapped around my throat.

Was Regulus attracted to that girl Arizona had mentioned? Had he kissed her? Was he dating her?

Arizona shoved him out of the doorway. "Dude, I'm

freezing here." Arizona maneuvered around Regulus's still body in the doorway. He leaned forward and gave me a hug. Although I generally avoid the touchy feely stuff, I let Arizona give me a friendly squeeze.

"Look what I brought," Arizona said, holding a piece of mistletoe high in the air.

"In your dreams," I said and shoved his arm with a laugh.

Dad stood framed in the kitchen doorway. He smiled at Arizona, then looked at Regulus. "Son, come on in." My stomach twisted when I heard him say 'son.' He hadn't done that before. I didn't think Dad had cared very much for Regulus while we dated.

I stepped back from the door, embarrassed at the ogling that I'd vowed to never do again with Regulus. Biscuit, who had been glued to Dad's side begging for food in the kitchen, ran to the door to greet our visitors. He ran circles around them in that happy dog way.

"I'm glad you both could come. At such short notice and everything." Arizona travelled across the family room, peering around corners. Regulus's direct stare sent tingly warmth to my face.

"Where is the Christmas tree?" Arizona scouted ahead.

"No tree." I answered. "We didn't do that this year."

Dad came forward and took Arizona's coat and held out his hand for Regulus's. "It's my fault. Mia said she didn't care whether we had one or not, so we didn't."

Arizona looked like a kid who'd lost his best friend.

"I thought everyone put one up at Christmas. I was looking forward to it." He flopped into Dad's recliner.

Dad gave me a look. His face said that he thought Arizona was a single digit on the IQ scale. I grinned.

I walked over and examined the buttons on the remote control. "Wanna check out my new game?" It was better than standing near Regulus. At least I could breathe easier with some distance between us.

"I thought that the dorms closed over the holidays." Dad perched for a moment on the arm of the couch. He folded his arms and examined Regulus, still standing near the door. Biscuit waited at Regulus's feet.

"There are a few students who get permission to stay." Regulus strode forward and took a seat at the opposite end of the couch from me while keeping the box he'd brought with him in his lap. Biscuit followed Regulus and jumped to sit on the sofa beside him. Regulus stroked the top of Biscuit's head.

"I'm really glad you guys came. All she seems to do is stay in her room and play Quest of Zion. She needs to socialize." My dad pivoted, returning to the kitchen before I could do anything more than groan.

I yelled over my shoulder. "Thanks a lot, Dad. You've painted me as the town recluse. Give me a hunchback, why don't you?" I clicked buttons on the remote until the menu came on. I needed the diversion to calm myself and the fluttering in my belly.

"Are you going to ask Regulus about the present?" Arizona hopped out of Dad's recliner and sat beside me on the sofa. He pointed at the box in Regulus's lap as though I wouldn't know which one he meant.

I tried to ignore him. "So, you guys must be the only ones still at the dorms. Anytime I've driven near campus during the holidays, it's been dead. Don't you get to go *home* sometimes?" I stressed the word *home* and tried to make my meaning clear without saying, in case my dad was listening. As in a not out-of-state, but out-of-dimension home.

"The present." Arizona sighed, arching his brows. "Give it to her."

"I can wait." Regulus's voice was even and unhurried. "We have no need to travel. And there *is* a need to continue observations for that project I'm working on this year."

"What project?" I glanced at him, my heart pumping a million gallons of blood to face. I imagined the bimbo that Arizona had mentioned last week. The one working on some class report with Regulus. If he thought for one second that I would listen to that—

"The project you said you would help us with. We're depending on you." He said the words in a low tone. My dad would have needed bionic hearing to catch the answer, but Regulus was being careful. And I was not.

Our eyes locked.

I clamped my lips together and turned my attention back to the television screen. I had devised a plan to avoid Regulus and Arizona and their constant secret mission agenda to save the world from interdimensional terrorism. And now it was time to put that plan in motion.

"Mmm...yeah. Well, I have so much going on right now."

I needed a break. A long break that didn't include romance or heartache or being held at gunpoint.

Chapter Three

Personal Space

"I can see how you're too busy to help your friends." Regulus's voice held a hint of sarcasm. So unlike his usual, straightforward manner, his tone was a mental slap. "Gaming, hanging out with Austin..."

Arizona grinned. His eyes ping ponged from me to Regulus and waited for the return.

Regulus was making me angry. The happy-go-lucky look on Arizona's face made me angry. I was brimming over with anger. We were supposed to be friends.

Evidently, my angry cup runneth over.

I forced my lips to curve up in a smile, hoping it looked better than it felt. It was an exhausting task to fake cheerful. Whoever had said 'Fake it till you make it,' must have dropped dead of exhaustion.

"It's a special present," Arizona said. "Please, Mia.

Don't be spiteful." His expression looked as earnest as a five-year-old's.

I shot him a squinty evil-eye that I normally reserved for drivers who cut me off in traffic. "I am not being spiteful. Here." I held out my hand and fluttered my fingers. "I'll open it. OK?"

I could play nice.

"Good." Regulus smiled, showing his perfect white teeth. OK, maybe not perfect. There was the tiny overlap on one left eyetooth. But that was me searching for imperfections. Who was I kidding?

The box was wrapped in brown paper with a large red bow taped awkwardly in the center. "You wrap this yourself?" The pressure of not knowing the contents of the box turned my tone sharp. I steadied my nervous hands against the sides of the gift. *Please don't let the gift be personal.*

"I did," Regulus said, almost grinning.

I refused to look up. I removed the red bow and ribbon after some effort. There had to be an entire roll of tape holding the paper onto the box. I picked along the edge of the transparent tape with my recently chewed fingernail.

"Next time, tape a small bomb on the top, and I'll defuse it. It would be easier than getting this tape off." I glanced up and saw that he was frowning. I'd hurt his feelings. *Great.* I'd finally succeeded in sounding like one of the mean girls with too much self-esteem or not enough. Guys wrapping presents should be outlawed.

Arizona crowded to sit beside me. He didn't seem to understand the unspoken rules of personal space. He reached for the package.

"I have a life span that is expiring as I wait." Arizona ripped paper off the package, exposing a shoe box.

I took it back from him. "I can get it now. Thanks." I lifted the lid. Crumpled newspaper sprang up from the interior.

"What is it?" I dug my hand inside to retrieve the surprise. My fingers closed around a slender metal object.

"Careful." Regulus rose to his feet.

I pulled a cell phone from the shroud of paper. The phone looked very similar to my current phone but lighter in weight. It was also pink. I'd hated pink from the moment I'd realized I was a girl, opting instead to follow my older brother's lead on everything. I looked from the phone to Regulus.

Arizona scooted closer to me. "It's not *only* a cell phone," he said, hinting like a game show host. "Guess what else it is?"

Looking from his eager face to Regulus's more guarded one, I answered. "Um. It has games and apps?" Regulus's eyebrows drew together and he seemed to wait for more.

"Thank you very much. I don't have anything for you. I don't usually exchange gifts with my...uh...friends." I put the phone back into the box.

They both watched me.

"You can use it as a phone. You'll have it with you all the time. You can also use it if..." Regulus turned to look toward the kitchen. "If you need to protect yourself."

"By calling *you*?" That wasn't going to happen.

"No." Regulus moved to sit on his haunches with

his knees almost touching mine.

The space between us seemed to shrink, trapping me and making my breathing shallow. He was too close. I could tolerate conversation with the ex, but touching would take me straight out of the friend zone and into torment city.

He leaned forward and whispered. His breath warmed the side of my cheek. "It's your own stunner. Yours. Arizona said it's what you wanted most."

He drew back but not far enough. I stared into dark blue eyes that always studied and analyzed. What did he see now? Did he see a silly girl who had once wanted her own weapon?

Breathe. I could smell his soap, a mix of clean male and citrus. A warm yellow glow of color vibrated from his body. I cursed my affinity for mixing sensory reactions. I'd been born seeing colors when I smelled. Smelling vanilla and wood tones when I heard a song on the radio. Picking up a bad taste in my mouth when I touched a random object.

Everything had been bearable until Regulus had come along. We'd only dated for a few months, but I'd spent every moment thinking about him. I obsessively checked my phone for missed calls. Planned time alone with him. Dreamed about his kisses. Replayed things he'd said.

For the first time ever, I worried if a guy thought I was pretty or fun or smart. I was *that* girl. And I foolishly thought we had a future together.

Synesthetes should never fall in love. It messed up the logic part of the brain and made you a stick of sensory dynamite waiting for a spark to set it off.

Regulus stood, took two steps back and tucked

both hands in his pockets.

Arizona put his hand on my arm. "Mia, you OK?"

"Sure." I nodded my head to confirm. "You know, guys, I really don't need this."

Regulus folded his arms over his chest and stepped back again, widening the distance between us to something I found acceptable. He actually had the nerve to look hurt.

I lowered my eyes from his arms to the jeans that hung low on his hips. His sweater had pulled up at the waist and I focused on the bit of skin I could see to avoid being hypnotized by his gaze. I realized he was probably wondering what I was staring at and heat flushed my face.

Looking at anything but him suddenly became the most important agenda for the evening.

I blinked and stared at my cell phone. "I'll figure it out later. For now—"

The doorbell rang.

"I'll get it." I exhaled and thought about gifts from the universe and perfect timing.

The visitor at the door began knocking like a drummer in a quick, rhythmic beat.

"Geez. I'm coming already." I hurried the last two steps to the door. Biscuit was already there, giving the unknown visitor his most menacing guard dog growl. I picked him up and used the other hand to open the door.

I breathed a sigh of relief to see my best friend Em. She resembled a model in a department store ad, clutching a huge Christmas bag to her chest. Behind her stood Tiny and Austin. Tiny was new to our group, a computer guru of Viking proportions.

Austin was my other best friend, a charming extrovert liked by everyone except Regulus.

"If it isn't Santa Claus and the Elves. I've never been so happy to see you guys."

Em stood in the doorway with her typical cheery grin until she peered over my shoulder and spotted Regulus. She lifted her brows at me and tilted her head. Then she looked at Austin to see his reaction. He mirrored the same expression. It might have been comical in other circumstances.

Em turned and handed the red and green Christmas sack to Austin. "Can you take this inside? Mia can help me get the food from the car."

Austin, his warm, caramel eyes twinkling with mischief, pretended to topple over from the weight of the bag. He glanced up at Tiny who towered above both of them. "Bag's full of coal. At least she didn't ask me to carry her purse."

Em grabbed my arm and dragged me toward her. "I need some assistance," she said, a smile decorating her face.

Tiny and Austin went inside as I walked out. I shrugged Em's hold from my arm and followed her to the shiny red car.

"So, you invited Regulus?" Em opened her car door.

"Yeah. I mean, as a friend sort of invitation..."

She lowered her chin, peering up at me with her I-know-your-innermost-secrets look. "If you say so."

I rolled my eyes. "Are we going to stand out here and freeze?"

Em handed over a stack of plastic containers. "Here. My mom thinks you and your dad need holiday food." She bent down to retrieve a casserole dish and straightened with it in her hand. "And somebody left you a tin of fruitcake on your porch."

"Ah, thanks." I took the casserole dish and stacked lighter containers on top. "I didn't expect you to come. Aren't both sets of your grandparents at your house?" I led the way back to my door and retrieved the fruitcake tin on the porch. "How did you escape?"

"I not only escaped, but I get to stay late. My great-aunt and uncle came as a surprise. They brought their three German Shepherds with them. They're sleeping in my room. My mom is stressed to the max and she said I could stay a while. Not the entire night. My sister will be ready to open presents at daybreak and will kill me if I'm not back."

Em opened the door for us and we stepped inside to hear laughter. Austin and Tiny were standing in front of the television discussing my new game system.

Dad noticed that Em and I had our arms full and rose from his chair.

"No, we've got it." I shook my head. "Em and I will put the food up."

In the small kitchen, we placed the containers on the bar. I lifted the plastic lid of the casserole dish to see a concoction of eggs and hash browns.

"That's for the morning. My mom said to heat it at 350 degrees—"

"We know how to warm food." I smirked at the way Em tried to take care of us.

"Mia only knows Microwaving 101 so she needs those instructions." Austin slung his dark hair out his eyes.

"Hey, Mr. Smarty, guy who lives on cold cereal. I am an expert at heating things." I faked a hurt look.

"Baby, I'll help you heat things up any day of the week." A wicked gleam and wide smile made me wish I had the hots for him. What was wrong with me?

"Mia doesn't need any help from you." Regulus's low voice menaced from behind my back.

I whirled around and my errant mouth engaged. "I'll heat things up with anyone I like." If he could study with some college girl, he had no right to say anything to me. I'd stepped into the role of the jealous ex—searching for the right hurtful words.

My shame increased ten-fold when I saw his face. I knew that look. I'd seen it on myself in the mirror. In private. In secrecy. Alone. Hurt that shouldn't be out there for others to witness. Was it pride? Or did he think he could claim me as his girl until the IIA swooped in and erased his memory again?

He turned his back on me and left the room.

Nothing in my seventeen years competed with this painful feeling—growing up without a mother, missing my older brother when he left...nothing.

Love sucked.

Chapter Four

Regulus

The smell of Christmas consisted of evergreen and baked goods. Cinnamon and burning logs. Warmth wrapped up with a shiny bow on top announcing love and goodwill.

Or so Regulus had been told in training.

Here, the chilly reception from Mia iced his holiday expectations. In his years of living in The Vault, he had followed a calendar with little interest. Each day held promise, but special days—holidays—didn't exist in his world.

He'd never understand the reason to mark a day on the calendar.

His gaze lingered on the Christmas cards strung across the living room mantle. Cards with Christmas trees, religious emblems, the fat man in the red suit.

The sound of footsteps made him grimace.

"I'm glad you're here," Emily said, her voice friendly. She stood at his right and looked at the cards.

"Hmm." Regulus didn't look away from the cards. After an awkward silence, he added, "Mia's not."

"She is." Emily glanced at the kitchen where Mia stood talking with Austin and Tiny.

"She doesn't laugh and talk with me like she does with Austin."

"You're not really jealous, are you?"

"No." He inched closer to the wood mantle and picked up a card picturing Santa's legs hanging from a chimney.

"Mia's known Austin forever. I mean, like since kindergarten."

He sensed Emily's stare. A stare meant to invite conversation. She called it *sharing.* Closing the card, he wished she'd find something else to do. He opened another card and stared at the meaningless scrawl.

"Regulus, look at me."

He dropped his hand from the Christmas card and sighed. "Yes, Emily."

"You'd better call me Em if I'm going to give you relationship advice. You used to call me Em."

"Em."

"Better." She chuckled and shook her head. "Be her friend. That's what she wants right now. See how she treats Austin? They're great friends."

"Em." He cleared his throat and thought about his words. "I don't know how to be her friend. I don't want to be her friend. If I knew how—"

"We're friends...talking all friendly-like."

"That's because I don't want to kiss your neck and run my hands along the curves of your body. I'm not thinking about—"

"OK," she said, drawing out the word, her eyes wide. "Awkward. Reg, it's not cool to tell somebody that. I give you kudos for the honesty thing, but rule number one is that you don't publicly announce your, um, thoughts in that direction."

He suppressed a sigh. "Since you are giving me advice, I thought you should completely understand the dilemma. I'm telling you what I've thought about telling her."

"No. And double no. She will run screaming from the room at that."

"Why would she not want the truth?"

Emily closed her eyes, took a deep breath, opened her eyes and pursed her mouth for a moment. "Here's the deal. You really hurt her."

"It was not intentional."

"Hey, I never said it was your fault. That memory cleanse thing sure does a number on relationships."

He looked away, not wanting to see her judgment. The IIA did things that were necessary. He'd never questioned their actions in the past. It made him uneasy that he was questioning them now.

"You think I should stay away from her."

"Gah. You are such a guy. Can you listen? I'm telling you to slow down if you want to start over with her. It's nice if there's a little trust before you do the hand-running-over-the-body scenario. And there has to be some honesty. A guarantee that the IIA won't do this to you again."

He watched her raise both brows. She wanted confirmation. He couldn't give her that.

"I know what I want," he said. "Your society is dishonest."

He noticed that she wasn't losing the disgusted expression—her nose wrinkled, her lip curled.

"I have a lot of work to do with you on the advice thing," she said.

"I didn't ask for it."

"Too bad. Mia's my friend and we look out for each other."

Mia stood in the kitchen giving them covert glances. He didn't mind. He wanted—no, he needed—her eyes on him. What he really wanted was that sparkle in her eyes that he'd seen with the others.

Mia's face seemed pale and her brown eyes luminous against her skin. Was she upset?

Since the memory cleanse, he searched for facts about his time with Mia. She'd mention something that he couldn't remember. Later, a touch or a smell or a sound would trigger emotions he couldn't understand. He hadn't forgotten about Emily. She continued to be bossy and interfering.

Emily waved a hand in front of his face. "Attention back on me, Romeo."

"Mia puts up these shields." Emily spoke and looked into the kitchen. "Shields that people erect after having life throw them one crappy curveball after another. She idolized her brother and then one day he was just gone. And I can't even get started on her mother."

Regulus heard Mia laughing at something. The pleasing tone of her throaty laugh warmed him like sitting near a campfire. He wished it had been at something he'd said.

Austin walked into the room with a comfortable

swagger that made Regulus grind his teeth.

"Hey man." Austin stood in front of him. A knowing quirk to his lips irritated and challenged.

"We'll talk more later."

Regulus watched Emily walk away, leaving him alone with Austin. Maybe if he ignored the guy, he'd go away too.

"We need a bag of ice. Come on." Austin pulled keys from his pocket. Grabbing his coat that he'd slung onto the back of the sofa, he waited at the door.

"Ice." Regulus wondered if he could restrain himself. The urge to punch Austin could rise quickly.

"Yeah. It'll take twenty minutes. I'll drive fast. We can talk." Austin stepped closer for a second. "It's important," he whispered.

Everyone wanted to talk tonight. Everyone except the one person he wanted to talk to. Leaning against the kitchen bar, she studied them, her brow furrowed.

"I'll go." Regulus took his coat from the hall closet and followed Austin to the door.

Outside in the Jeep, he waited and Austin adjusted knobs, cranking up the heat and the music in unison. Austin drove away from the house. The woods thickened along the long driveway to the paved road. Oak and hickory trees hid the moonlight. Only the headlights pierced the cocoon of darkness.

"Our mad scientist Bleeker has called her."

"What do you mean, he called her? What exactly did he say? Turn around. We're going back to the house. She can't be a—"

"Hold on there, Kemosabi. She's fine. Her dad is there. Tiny's there. Your man Arizona is there. It won't make a difference if you're not there."

He wanted to punch Austin. "Continue."

"She won't talk to him. I mean, she answered the first time and hung up on him when he identified himself. Now, she's blocked his number." Austin turned the Jeep onto the road.

"Why didn't she tell me?" Regulus rubbed the back of his neck. She hadn't wanted him to know.

"I found out accidentally. She wasn't going to tell me either." Austin accelerated to highway speed. "I picked up her phone when it rang. Said 'block' on the screen. I asked her who she was blocking and she got this panicked look on her face. I knew something was wrong."

"I should have known about it. Immediately."

"She's in denial. If she pretends Dr. Bleeker doesn't exist, she doesn't have to deal with it. With you or the IIA."

He felt a deep ache in his gut that she'd put herself in danger. "The IIA can protect her."

"So, it's all about the IIA, huh?"

Regulus sat in silence, looking out his passenger window, his nerves stretched to a snapping point.

Austin didn't wait for an answer. "That's what I thought. Listen man. She's not the only one in denial. You'd better get your head on straight before this psycho does something...psychotic."

"It's time for this to end. I won't wait for directives. You can be sure of me."

"That's what I want to hear." Austin adjusted the bill of his ball cap and nodded, his face lit by the dashboard lights.

Chapter Five

Mistletoe

I stifled a laugh at Em's kindergarten squeal at the guys' return. "Did somebody spike Em's eggnog?"

She glided across the room to the front door like a ballerina from the Nutcracker. "Austin, Regulus. We've been waiting for you guys to get back." She hooked her arms around each, escorting them into the room.

"Huh?" Austin said.

Both guys gave her the girls-are-crazy look.

Em lugged the jumbo-sized Christmas bag beside her feet and reached inside it. Santa-like, she handed one gift to each person in the room, including Dad.

I squeezed my eyes shut and wrinkled my nose. "Ah, Em. No. We said we weren't doing this."

"Tell my mom that. She thinks shopping is a national sport and wants to train me to win the gold medal." Em smiled apologetically. "Don't be mad. See, you're not special. Everybody gets something."

Em surveyed the guys all shifting uncomfortably. "Open them. Now," she ordered. She sounded so much like her mother that it freaked me out.

We obeyed and opened our gifts. I lifted a six-pack of lip glosses from the bag. They were taped to a music download gift card. Em was trying hard to bring me into the world of cosmetics and this was a baby step.

"Very cool," I said, rotating the pack to read flavor names like Busta Red and Texty Tart. I had to temper my enthusiasm or she'd be begging to highlight my hair. Blonde is blonde. I failed to see what difference it would make.

I glanced around the room. Austin held up a gift that looked a lot like mine. He had a gift card with new ear buds for his iPod. Tiny pulled out a knit beanie and immediately took the one off his head to replace it with the new one. I chuckled because it appeared identical to the one he'd taken off. His red curls sprang from the edges of the cap.

Arizona sat staring at the gift in his hands. Regulus hadn't even opened his bag.

"What is it, Arizona?" I walked across the room to stand in front of him. "I couldn't tell from over there."

He placed the object back into the bag. Poof.

"Oh, no you don't," I said. "I want to see. Come on."

"He doesn't have to show it if he doesn't want to," Em said in a what-were-you-thinking tone.

Arizona, who always had something to say, was speechless. "I'd rather not. It's something special."

I shrugged and avoided Regulus on my way back to the ottoman seat. I uncapped the tube of Love Ya Lollipop and tentatively swiped the rosy gloss across my lower lip. Then I rubbed my lips together like Em had shown me. I lifted my chin and met Regulus's intense stare. His gaze traveled to my mouth. My stomach coiled in an inverted roller-coaster loop, leaving my palms sweaty from the G-force. I stopped rubbing my lips together.

"Emily, thank you for being so thoughtful." My dad waved another gift card. "This is my favorite bookstore."

"No problem, Mr. Taylor. You're my second Dad." She jumped up to run, then hugged him. "You let me eat junk and stay up all night. I just realized," she said, putting one finger to her chin in mock thought, "that you are my link to normalcy."

Dad laughed. He put his finger to his lips in a shushing gesture. "Shh. That's supposed to be our secret." He rose with the bag and card in hand. "Now that Mia has you for company, I'm going to head upstairs and indulge in some reading. You guys stay as long as you want."

"Night, Mr. Taylor." Several voices melded into one farewell greeting.

"So what's in the bag?" Tiny asked and leaned toward Arizona. "We're all friends here, right?"

Tiny was far from being Mr. Manners. Everybody was getting along so far. A dark thundercloud of tension moved into the room.

"Hey, Arizona can keep a gift private if he wants." I held up the new game controllers. "Who wants to play?"

Arizona cleared his throat. "I don't mind showing it. I didn't know if Em wanted everyone to know what she gave me." He pulled the gift from the bag.

I could tell it was a picture frame. He turned the frame around to display the front. It was a candid photo from the winter formal. A lump the size of a s'mores worthy marshmallow formed in my throat. I swallowed past the bitter lump.

"That's a fantastic shot." I walked back across the room to get a better look and examined Em and Arizona in their formalwear. "You guys looked..." I didn't finish my sentence. Regulus moved closer and studied it as well. He stood an inch away, our arms touching as he leaned in.

"What's this in the background?" Regulus cocked his head to one side. This question pointedly reinforced the fact that he hadn't been there. That he'd stood me up.

"It was a Grimm's Fairy Tales theme or something like that," Em said. "I thought Arizona might like to have a memento for his dorm room. So, everybody, let's move along. We have better things to do than stare at this picture."

I backed away slowly to retreat to the safety of my ottoman. How many times would I mentally relive the worst night of my life? Obviously once more.

The television murmured low in the background. Tiny stifled a yawn and used the remote control to flip though the channels. A headline banner, 'Breaking News,' appeared on the screen and I motioned at Tiny.

"Turn it up a little." I froze as the television displayed the Goliath city limits sign.

"The citizens of Goliath are shaken by this latest discovery. Just last week, an elderly woman discovered a decomposed body in her compost bin. Now, this quiet Southern town is facing a second murder. A body has been discovered in the basement of the pharmaceutical lab destroyed in a recent fire. Both crimes are under investigation." The video footage of a burned building cut to a Santa Claus. "In happier holiday news…"

Tiny muted the television.

"So, the dead body…is that Bleeker's work?" Austin addressed me. Everyone in the room examined me in courtroom jury anticipation. Austin continued, "The body in the lab makes sense. Did our evil Dr. Bleeker put a body in that lady's compost bin? Another experiment gone wrong?"

"Hello." I singsonged the words as loud as possible and held up my hand. "We're not the crime squad. Students. I am a student. Card-carrying certified student. Goliath can take care of its own crime."

"We have a responsibility to make sure this doesn't happen again." Regulus sat back on the sofa with his arms folded, engaging me in a stare-down.

"We? You have a mouse in your pocket? We does not include me. Or anyone else in this room."

Regulus softened his voice and one corner of his mouth tipped up. A smile that didn't reach his eyes. "It doesn't matter how you feel about me—"

"Not here. Not now." I shook my head and broke eye contact. OK, so he'd won the staring contest. My breathing quickened and I pulled my hair off my perspiring neck.

Em appeared at my side, holding a tray of cookies.

I picked up a sugary confection and smiled at her. "Thanks."

Arizona's eyes sparkled and he grabbed a reindeer-shaped cookie. Examining the pretzel antlers, he said, "You are a genius." He ate half a reindeer face with one bite.

"You can have Rudolf," she said, handing one to Regulus.

Regulus pretended to study the cookie for moment. He looked up and our eyes met. "Sorry," he mouthed.

Diversion? Diversion. I turned to Em. "So, how did your mom like the purse you ordered from Macy's?"

Later, everyone was either talking or eating. I gathered a couple of small gifts my dad had given me and the gift from Em and made my way upstairs. I put the boxes on my desk and turned to leave my room when I ran into someone.

"Hey!" I backed away from the wall of Regulus's chest. "Say something or stomp when you follow me. You scared the bejesus out of me."

He gave me a bashful smile that lifted his eyebrows in an apologetic fashion.

"You forgot this one."

He handed me his gift of the stunner/cell phone.

"Oh yeah. Thanks. I mean...I appreciate that you thought I needed a weapon."

"It wasn't that. I wanted to give you something special. Something that you desired." Rolling his shoulders forward, he tucked his hands into his pockets and examined his boots. He took a deep breath and met my eyes again after a long awkward silence.

"Well, whatever the reason, thanks." I moved forward to indicate that I was leaving my room. His uncertainty squeezed at my chest. Uncertainty that repelled my senses with a chalkboard scraping sound only I could hear. Synesthesia. Uncertainty rolling from him that made me want to cover my ears.

"We have this history, this chemistry," he said in a quiet voice. "I know it upsets you."

"No, you're wrong." I forced my voice to be light. Disinterested. "We dated, we broke up, we don't have a lot to talk about now."

"Hey, you guys are needed down here." Em called from the bottom of the stairs. I thanked the forces of ESP, divine intervention, or plain old good luck that she'd come to rescue me.

"Coming," I yelled.

Regulus took a deep breath. "We need to have this conversation. You saved my life in Goliath," he said. The words ran together in an urgent, bomb-defusing speed.

"And you saved mine. So, we're even." I turned sideways to edge around him since he blocked my doorway. I sucked in my breath, trying to make sure that my skin didn't touch his. He put a hand across the door frame and trapped me between freedom and his body.

"I am not trying to upset you. I want to understand why you hate me. I'm trying to be your friend. I didn't choose to have the memory cleanse."

"Yeah. I got that." I pushed against his arm blocking my way. He didn't budge.

"I don't understand why you keep pushing me

away," he whispered and let his arm fall.

My heart rate tripled. I didn't lift my head and forced my breathing to slow.

"Pushing away would imply that I care. I don't. See, you didn't study about this in that place—the Vault—but this is how it works. We date people, have fun, then we move on. It's the way we do things here." I made the mistake of looking up. Regulus's hurt expression knotted my stomach. I walked away before he could see me fighting tears.

Everything about him pulled me in—his strength, his honesty, his awkwardness. Breaking my ties with him felt like pouring alcohol over my deep emotional cut. A personal cleansing I needed for self-protection.

* * *

We played video games until midnight. Austin and Tiny were the first ones to leave. I waved into the darkness, watching them hop into Austin's jeep. A sliver of moonlight illuminated Austin's grin. Tiny turned the radio volume up and a guitar riff broke the silence.

Behind me, Em giggled. Her happiness smelled of pink, sugary bubblegum with a hint of salt. I turned to see Arizona holding the mistletoe he'd brought. He dangled it over Em's head. Their lips met in a movie-screen passionate kiss.

"Merry Christmas to you," Arizona said to Em.

Em opened her eyes and sighed.

"Oh, get a room." I swore under my breath at the scent of cinnamon hot lust that filled the space.

She looked guiltily at me and turned to Arizona.

"You'd better go. I have to be home in a few hours."

Arizona frowned. "OK." He picked up his Christmas gift and immediately began grinning. "Thanks for this."

Em smiled with him. They were ridiculous— kissing and flirting constantly. I wanted to warn her that happiness doesn't last. That it would weave a fantasy around her heart and magically disappear when she least expected it.

"You never opened yours," Em said to Regulus. "It's a book. I had to special order it from Amazon. *American Slang for the Tourist.* I thought it might come in handy."

Regulus nodded. "Thank you, but I'm not a tourist. I consider myself a dual citizen."

"Oh, I know. I thought, well, um..." Em said.

"Even dual citizens might find a new phrase." I looked at the grandfather clock that stood in the entry. "It's getting late."

Regulus and Arizona walked to the door, carrying their packages. Arizona opened the door and turned to Regulus. "Hey man, can you grab that package of cookies on the coffee table? Em's giving those to us."

Regulus turned back and retrieved the package. I watched him bend. His perfect butt was an unfair secret weapon. I mentally kicked myself for faltering. *Off-limits.* I scolded myself for thinking about him that way. Scolded myself for even letting my gaze travel his direction.

He strolled toward me and stared into my eyes. I thought maybe he had seen me checking him out when I felt something touch the top of my head. I broke eye contact and tilted my head up to see the mistletoe held by Em's fingers. When I lowered my head, Regulus was inches from my face.

"Kiss," Em said from behind me. "It's tradition. Go on."

I planned to kill her at those words. A slow death involving greenery and maybe a couple of Christmas ribbons.

Regulus leaned closer and I froze. Everything at that moment moved in slow motion. I saw the question in his eyes and the movement of his arms as he let them fall to his sides. He leaned down, his warm breath touched my face and I willed myself to move.

I didn't.

He didn't go for a deep kiss. I wouldn't have been able to stop that because my brain had given up sending signals to my muscles. All my energy powered my racing heart.

After his soft lips brushed mine, he paused then pulled away long enough for our noses to touch. My stomach knotted and tingled.

"Merry Christmas." And he was gone.

I blinked. He and Arizona had already stepped out the door and I could hear them starting their motorcycles. I'd officially morphed into a living, breathing zombie.

Em shut the door softly. "Hey," she said. "You OK?"

I rolled my head to loosen my tension-filled neck. "Sure. Fine. You shouldn't have done that." I walked back to the living room to pick up a platter of cookies. Carrying it to the kitchen, I stared straight ahead to avoid her.

She put her hand on my shoulder. "You are definitely not OK. You're freaking out. Stop walking."

I continued into the kitchen and set the cookie platter on the counter.

"I can't talk about this." I rushed back to the living room to collect some empty soda cans.

My want-the-boy-can't-have-the-boy moment worsened because Em put her arms around me in a consoling hug. She stared at me, leaning her head against mine before speaking. "I know Arizona told you that you can't date Regulus. That the IIA are watching for that. I don't care about their rules. The only important thing in life is love."

"Em, you've watched *The Notebook* too many times."

She blocked my path as I turned. "It's OK. It's going to be OK."

I blinked and swallowed. "I said I'm OK. How OK do I have to be?" I yelled.

I grabbed more empty soda cans and waited until she left the kitchen. Leaning over the sink, I cupped my hand under the faucet and splashed cold water onto my face and neck.

Why wouldn't my friends let me get back to the way it was before? Before my emotions held me hostage in a cyclone of hurt?

We didn't talk like we usually did while cleaning up after the party. Em knew me better than anyone and she knew a conversation would mess me up. The mistletoe was evil. Pure holiday wretchedness.

My stomach churned at the betrayal.

We stood on the dark porch step. "I'm sorry," she said, holding both my hands and pulling me in for a hug. I buried my face in her humongous scarf.

"I know. I know. But you can't fix this. So stop."

I walked her to the car and stood in the darkness, watching her leave until the taillights disappeared.

I hugged my arms to my body, feeling alone and hopeless. The wind whistled a lonely tune through the pines—a soundtrack for my life. The suspended swing creaked, an eerie squeaky sound from the chains. Biscuit give a low growl from behind me.

"Shh. It's only the wind," I cooed.

A man crept toward me from the shadows.

Chapter Six

Pete

"Hey Sunshine." Pete knew he'd startled her by the drop of her mouth, the widening of her eyes, her quick intake of breath. It gave him an odd feeling that Mia didn't expect to see him again. Ever.

"Pete?" Mia said his name with a disbelieving lilt at the end. Her mouth made an 'O' and she put one shaky hand against the porch's stone wall. She had the look of a lottery winner, all smiles and don't-wake-me-if-I'm-dreaming. "Is it really you?"

Her voice washed him in light and goodness and the smell of peanut butter. She smelled like she'd bathed in peanut butter and honey, but he knew it was only his synesthesia at work. They'd both been blessed—or cursed if you asked some synesthetes.

Only five feet separated them. She squinted at him in his dark coat, dark pants, dark everything. He was accustomed to blending into the background. He moved a little closer and set down his duffel bag, thunking with more than one night's change of clothes.

Her face opened into a toothy grin that threatened to overtake her face. A goofy grin he remembered well. He'd last seen her in secret, in the hospital, in a real mess.

She wasn't out of trouble, but she didn't know it. She couldn't know or she wouldn't be standing on the porch alone.

He closed the distance in two giant steps and pulled her into a crushing hug that said he missed her. They'd never hugged when they'd been young. A hug usually ended in a *half-Nelson* that merited scolding from their dad.

She sniffled and pulled back.

"Hey there. No crying. You're acting like you thought I was dead. Come on—"

She rubbed one hand under her eye and slugged him on the bicep. Hard. She grimaced and rubbed her fist. "What are you doing here? Have you come home for good? Why did you—"

"Shush. Dad up?" He pivoted in a one-eighty to study the woods, and finally looked back at her face.

"No, probably not. He went upstairs hours ago. But you'd better wake him." She studied the duffel bag. "You are staying, right?"

"Yes." He picked up the bag and led the way inside. "I've stood outside for the last half hour, trying to come up with a believable story for Dad."

"Hope it's a good one. As a matter of fact, it'll need to be stellar. Like there was an alien abduction and they just landed the mother ship to return you. No, that won't work. They'd have returned you way before now."

"Smartass." He goosed her side with one finger.

"I thought I was Sunshine," she said, her voice wobbly. One fat tear slipped down her cheek.

He pretended not to see and busied with taking off his coat and gloves. "I missed you. More than you know."

She nearly knocked him over with another linebacker-style hug from the side.

"Hey, easy there." He kissed the top of her head. "You're quite a bit stronger than the old days. You might hurt me."

She smirked and sniffled again. "Oh, funny. You've bulked up." She reached over and squeezed his bicep. "I didn't know you had muscles."

"And you're not a little girl anymore. When did you grow up?"

She blushed and took his hand in a vise-grip and led the way to the kitchen. Releasing him, she pointed at the barstool. "I can't believe you've been outside for that long. Tell me the real story and not the one you're telling Dad."

"We can talk later. Right now I've got to face Dad."

She frowned with the same irritated look she always gave him. The one that said she was going to argue. But she didn't.

"OK. But I have questions that you'd better answer."

He leaned on both elbows and examined platters of candy and cookies. "These look great."

"Don't try to divert my attention." She leaned forward on the counter across from him. "You're giving off nervous vibes like a freaky glowworm."

"Can't fool you. You can read me like a walking billboard."

"Don't get me wrong for saying this. I've been waiting for the day you'd come home. Dad needs to know you're alive. But what's going on? Why home now?"

"It was an emergency," he said.

"What?"

"I asked to be sent home. We received intel that Bleeker is planning something. He's watching you."

The reason for his return ruined the simple childlike pleasure she'd shone at seeing him on the porch. He could see it in her face. He smelled her fear, felt it vibrate.

"Oh?" She evened out her tone and added a hint of indifference. "Can I make you something to drink? You drink coffee, right?"

Now, she was diverting the conversation to a safer topic.

"Yeah. That'd be nice. Coffee with creamer."

"OK. Anything you want. This is going to make Dad's Christmas." Mia scooped out some cocoa mix into a mug. Grabbing the milk from the fridge, she turned her head, staring at him like she was afraid he'd disappear.

He didn't respond.

"Having you home is like the best present I could get. I haven't breathed a word to anyone. Not that you were alive. That I'd seen you. Well, except my friends who know..." Her hands shook when she poured the milk in a coffee mug.

"Sis, I'm so sorry that you got pulled into this.

When I left home, I did it for more than one reason. I thought if I removed myself from this location, from you and Dad... Well, I was naive. I thought I could keep this away from you." He shook his head.

"You didn't create portals. This mess isn't your fault."

"Yeah. I know that's logical, that I didn't bring this on us. But I feel responsible. I need to make sure you're safe."

"From the IIA?"

He arched a brow. "The IIA doing something I need to know about?"

She ignored him and took a couple of minutes before speaking again. She continued with the hot cocoa prep. Stirring powder, pushing buttons on the microwave. Watching her make coffee seemed so normal compared with discussing an agency from another dimension. "I don't know. Regulus keeps bringing up the fact—"

"You tell him to back off or if you don't want to talk to him, I'll take care of it." He picked Biscuit up and placed the dog on his lap.

"Are you going to tell me the truth about what you do?" She chewed her thumbnail and only stopped when the microwave beeped. She removed the steamy mug.

"I'll tell you what I can. I'm telling you because you have decisions to make. Decisions about the IIA. I didn't know they'd try to force you and I'd assumed you'd tell them to take a hike."

She didn't make eye contact. "I sorta went all swoony over their team leader. I went did a stupid girl thing. I'm smarter now."

He laughed. "People do stupid 'swoony' things. Human nature."

She snorted. "Oh, I'm sure I'd win some sort of crown for it."

"You have choices you don't even know of yet."

"Like what?"

"I was recruited for Operation Zodiac. OZ for short. It's a black op, a military unit that doesn't exist." He shouldn't even tell her that much.

"Like Call of Duty." The minute she said it, he could tell she regretted it. She probably expected him to laugh or roll his eyes, but it was too close to the truth. She continued. "So if this is so clandestine, how can you tell me about it?"

"That's all I'm telling you. And you won't tell. You don't have to know more."

"It's dangerous?"

He stared at her without blinking. "Every day."

"Then why did you join it? Why?" Her voice cracked and she wouldn't look him in the eyes.

"I had to, Mia. It was agree to work with the IIA, or join Operation Zodiac. Our guys."

"Oh. So, it's a matter of national allegiance."

"You're simplifying the issue. Mia—"

"You left us. We needed you."

"I know."

"No, you don't know."

He reached across and took her hands. Squeezed both in his. "I don't pretend to know what I did to you guys. But I did it to protect you both. Please forgive me."

Another fat tear slid down her cheek and hit the counter. He watched it fall and looked back into her eyes. Pain stabbed his chest. He'd seen her cry twice in one night. He couldn't remember ever seeing her cry that much. "I'd have done anything for you guys. Even leave you."

"It's a crazy life. Why does it have to be like this?"

"I don't know. 'Cause we crave high adventure?" He grinned at her.

She looked at him and raised her eyebrows. "Huh?"

"We train for this life. To be good at it."

"You are making zero sense."

"Quest of Zion. The agency that selects operatives for OZ uses the game." He ran a hand down his neck. Took off his coat. Grinned at her open mouth and the confused furrow between her brows.

"You're joking, right?"

"Not a bit."

He took a deep breath and looked down at the mug she'd put on the counter. "And I know my assignment is dangerous..." He kept the smile on his face. "But not as dangerous as trusting you to make coffee."

She frowned and looked at the mug. "Oh no, I've made you cocoa." She shook her head. "I was excited to see you. So fire me. Coffee. Yeah. Making coffee now." She slid the mug to herself and began to start the coffee maker.

Pete laughed and she joined him. They were laughing and grinning like old times. Then Mia's smile froze and he turned to see Dad, standing with a frown on his face.

Dad stood in flannel pajama bottoms and a T-shirt. He looked older. Tired.

"Pete?"

"Hi, Dad." Pete slid from the barstool. "I'm home."

Dad rushed forward and embraced him. The older man's shoulders shook and Pete lowered his head, not looking at Mia.

"I can't believe it. I can't believe you're alive and here."

His resolve to stay emotionally distant toppled like a teetering house of cards. Mia's evident relief at his homecoming, the pinnacle on top, his dad's wet cheeks, the base. His defenses were gone.

"I'm here. Merry Christmas, Dad."

* * *

He sat in the dark, alone in the room he'd spent the first eighteen years of his life. The bed seemed smaller. The posters on his wall, a juvenile tribute to the bands and videogames he loved. He picked up a photo from his desk. A teen stood next to a pretty girl in a swimsuit. He'd forgotten he'd even dated her.

It was like he'd traveled in a time machine. His room looked the same. His family acted as though he'd never left. He didn't regret anything that'd happened. Regrets wouldn't build a future, change the past, or force forgiveness. Forgiveness hadn't been granted tonight. He'd given his dad a story about running off to California to be with a girl he'd met online.

Eighteen-year-old kids did stupid things. It was an easy story to believe. He added in a story about drugs. Drugs from the girlfriend. And another story of being too ashamed to contact home.

But he'd told his dad that he was straight now. He'd said he had a job in California working for a small gaming company.

But the hurt went too deep for forgiveness after a few hours. The anger was there. It was the same he'd felt toward his mother when he'd seen her as an adult. Nancy Taylor had run away, taking his little boy heart with her, to a new life. His first thought had been to kill her when he'd discovered her. Actual murder. Then he'd come to his senses and considered things like prison and hell.

And he'd never really hated her. Not when he reached down deep inside, to that place where he could still remember her.

He was stronger than that.

But, he was thinking about killing again. Not that he was a bad person, but he didn't know how to stop Eli Bleeker any other way. And he now had authorization to do it.

The man and the genetics corporation called Aidos gambled that no one would stop them. Gambled that political agendas would get in the way.

But Bleeker didn't understand family.

Pete leaned against the headboard, cursing the fact that Dr. Eli Bleeker—criminal, sicko, and butcher—had made this personal.

Chapter Seven

Christmas Photos

I crawled into bed, tired and ready to crash. One second after placing my head on the pillow, I heard a ding from my cell phone. A text message appeared onscreen. It was Austin.

"Merry Christmas Babe. Hope u dreamed of sugar plum fairies and rock concerts. What time do u want me to come to ur house? Haven't been 2 bed yet. Played Quest all night. Is there more of Em's candy at ur house?"

"How did you know I was awake?" I texted and yawned.

"Gifted. U aren't only 1 with super powers."

"Ha."

"I see u r in bed."

"You're good. Can you see me putting the phone down and going back to sleep? Talk to you tomorrow."

I placed the phone on the nightstand and fluffed

my pillow. After fifteen minutes of tossing, I still wasn't asleep. I pushed my comforter off and walked over to my bedroom window. It was still dark outside, but the quarter-moon cast a dim light over the trees. No streetlamps meant I couldn't see the snow covered ground as well as I would like.

I pressed my face to the cold window in amazement. Thick piles of pristine snow covered the ground, unmarred like a smooth blanket.

My phone dinged with another text. I picked it up, expecting to see yet another note from Austin.

"Snow is beautiful." The text wasn't from Austin, but from Regulus.

"Yes." I sighed. We'd stopped texting weeks ago. It was almost like he knew I was thinking about him.

The phone dinged again and a picture popped up on the display. Probably taken from his dorm window at Whispering Woods University. The streetlights lit up the place. Large drifts of snow covered the parking lot. Not even one vehicle stood in the lot. Were Regulus and Arizona the only ones there?

Ding.

Another photo of Regulus and Arizona's motorcycles. That was a weird thing to photograph. But Regulus didn't always think the way I did.

I climbed back into bed and Biscuit entered my room, walking in a slow, sleepy trot. I'd made some noise and woken him. He leaped onto my bed and ducked his head under the covers.

Ding.

Regulus was as bad as Austin and needed to get some sleep. Snow was not that exciting. Or maybe it was an excuse to talk to me. I picked up my phone. This one was in his hallway. I couldn't pick out anything special and wondered why he would send it.

Ding.

I squinted at the next image; the photo was small and my eyes strained. In the right corner was a gloved hand. Why was he showing me this? I shot up in the bed, dislodging Biscuit in the process. The photo was dark, but I could see bunk beds in the background. I tapped in on the photo and made it larger. A person slept in the bottom one and a second person in the top. I recognized the striped comforters.

Regulus and Arizona in their bunk beds.

I got out of bed and found my shoes. No socks, no real clothes, no time. I shrugged on my heavy coat and called Arizona's number. I muttered hallelujah that I'd put him in my favorites call list.

"Pick up, pick up, pick up."

"Hello." His voice was groggy from the other end.

"There's someone in there. Wake up. Get up." I whisper-screamed.

"Is that you, Mia?"

"Yes, it's me. Get up. Someone is in your room." I didn't need argument or calm reassurance. I needed action.

I heard Regulus's voice in the background. "Is she OK?"

"I've got the lights on. It's just us." Arizona sounded irritated. "Did you have a bad dream?"

"No. I didn't." I sat on the edge of my bed, unsure if someone was going to kill them or not.

"We're fine. Why would you think someone was in here?" Arizona said. His voice teased.

Maybe someone had a gun pointed at his head and he couldn't tell me.

"Hi. It's me." Regulus had taken Arizona's phone. "What scared you?"

"Where is your phone?" My voice cracked.

He paused. "Just a minute."

I waited and Biscuit nuzzled my back.

Regulus cleared his throat. "I don't know. I always leave it on my dresser." I heard the sleepiness leaving his voice by the end of his sentence.

"Someone sent me pictures from your phone. The last photo has a hand in it. Are you sure no one is in there? Do I need to come over?"

He laughed, but the sound had a nervous edge that he couldn't hide. "Pictures of a hand?" After a minute of silence, he spoke, "You've been in these rooms. There is nowhere to hide. Wait a minute." Seconds passed. "Checked the bathroom. Nobody."

"I'm coming. This doesn't feel right. I can call campus security."

I heard Arizona ask for his phone. "We've got this," Arizona said in a voice that sounded much more alert.

"But—"

"Mia, it's Christmas. Your dad will be getting up soon. I'll text you as soon as we figure out what's going on."

"OK," I said in a resigned voice. I hadn't even told them about Pete.

I tapped END and took off my coat and shoes. I wondered if Pete was already asleep. I climbed back into bed where Biscuit happily snuggled.

I knocked once softly on the wall that separated my headboard from Pete's.

A soft echoing rap made me smile.

I thought about Regulus and the photos. My thoughts forced a shiver through my body. "I have a bad feeling about this," I said to Biscuit. "Whoever had his phone could have easily killed them."

Biscuit didn't answer. He was tired of me talking.

I hadn't shut my curtains and rays of morning sunlight streamed into my room. Fat snowflakes thickened into a whirl of white outside my window.

Ding.

My hand shook as I picked up my phone. An image of my house and my bedroom window stared back at me.

I ran and looked out my window. Footprints marred the perfect snow below.

* * *

Snow blanketed the ground in a postcard setting. Although we didn't get up until mid-morning, Dad made biscuits accompanied by chocolate gravy and popped the casserole from Em's mom into the oven. He played Christmas music and we sang along. Dad and I had saved one gift apiece to be opened. Pete played Santa and brought out his gifts for us.

Having Pete home made us giddy.

We lounged on the sofa with our feet perched side by side on the coffee table. Dad sat in his recliner watching *It's a Wonderful Life* for the one-millionth time.

I checked my cell phone constantly for a text from Arizona. I was a minute away from texting him when he sent a message.

"Someone has stolen Regulus's cell phone. See you soon."

The lack of information was enough to remind me that I shouldn't care. If they didn't want me to know, it didn't matter, because I needed to distance myself from the IIA and especially from Regulus.

"What are you frowning about?" Pete asked.

"Nothing." Although I wanted to tell him, I was scared. I'd trust Pete with anything. But if I told him, he would think he needed to take action. And I knew that was the reason he'd returned.

I didn't want him taken away from me.

The text reminded me of the present upstairs from Regulus that I had dismissed so easily. Dad wouldn't accept my offer to clean up the kitchen so I ran to my room, taking the stairs two at a time. The box sat where Regulus had left it last night.

I lifted the cell phone from its nest of paper and held my breath, wondered how easily the weapon function triggered. My own stunner. Last fall, I had asked for one during training with Regulus and been told no. An emphatic no. A you'll-shoot-your-eye-out no. That was back when I thought I would be a permanent addition to Regulus's team. Now the answer had changed from no. Regulus didn't realize that hell would sell snow cones before I'd join the IIA now.

Powering it on, I could see that it was a match for the functions of my current cell phone. I wondered how IIA agents got their weapons. Did the IIA make this for me? Knowing that I wouldn't be satisfied until I could try out the stunner features, I tiptoed downstairs. If I could slip outside for a minute alone, I could aim it at a tree or rock.

I stood on the third from the bottom step when I heard Dad's raised voice. He was angry at someone. His tone was different from any he'd ever used with me.

"I think it's in poor taste to pick today to suddenly call. Honestly, you can't expect Mia to welcome you into her life after all these years. She doesn't even know you." My dad's voice shook, each word biting the ear of the listener.

Silence.

"Well, that's not how it works. This call will upset her and she's been depressed over a boyfriend lately... No... No..."

More silence and I could hear Dad pacing.

"I didn't say you couldn't talk to her ever. It's just not going to be today. This is bad timing. I also find it odd that you wouldn't ask about our son."

I could hear his uneven breathing.

"What is it that you really want? You've never called before." Pause. "Yes, it is my business. I am the one who raised her."

The oven door slammed. The smell of burning food filled the air.

"You are being ridicu—"

I heard Dad put the phone down. The call had ended.

I stepped softly to the front door where I slipped outside. Leaning against the door, I stood on the porch and momentarily forgot about the weapon in my hand.

Nancy Taylor had wanted to talk to me, her daughter. That was a nice change from trying to kill me. Dad had no idea the phone call was loaded. Loaded with evil possibilities. What did she really want?

Surveying the blanket of white on the ground, I caught a glimpse of a familiar wooden structure at the end of my long gravel driveway. The pink stunner felt exactly like my cell phone with its lightweight case. I pointed at the little shelter I called my waiting booth and directed a mental command to shoot. I visualized the edge of the roof coming down. And then it did.

"Yahoo," I squealed before realizing how loud my voice would be. Dad and Pete appeared at the front door to see me jumping up and down in glee.

"Mia?" Dad looked around. "Are you alone? Did you see something?"

"Oh. The snow. I was excited about the snow." I threw my arms around him. "It's cool, isn't it?"

He looked at me with raised brows and a pursed mouth. "Get inside before you freeze."

Pete shook his head and gave me a playful pat to the back of my head.

Chapter Eight

Where Oh Where

One self-induced sugar coma later, I moaned at the caller ID on my cell phone. My screen read, 'Blocked call.'

Didn't psychos take a break on the holidays?

"Biscuit?" I shuffled downstairs and through the house in my new bunny slippers. One floppy ear had been chewed already. Jealous dog.

"I let him out earlier," Pete said. "He needed some fresh air."

"It's too cold."

"Cold for you. Not cold for a dog." Pete sat on a stool at the bar. He concentrated on his laptop screen and didn't look up at me.

I peered through the opening in the kitchen curtains, searching for Biscuit. He usually stayed near the fence.

"He'll come to the door when he's ready." Pete

reached to the cookie plate nearest him, popped a macaroon into his mouth, then chewed once. "You make these?"

"No. Em."

He grabbed a paper towel and covered his mouth with it. "Good. This tastes horrible." He spit cookie into the towel.

I cracked the door and stuck my head outside. "Biscuit!"

"I want to talk to you about some things. Will you stick around here so we can spend some time together?" Pete cleared his throat. "You listening?"

"Uh-huh. Biscuit!" I yelled.

"Mia, this is important."

"My dog freezing is important, too." I looked around for my boots. "I'm going outside." I stepped out of the slippers and into my insulated boots.

"Did you hear a word I said? I said you can't—"

"Be right back. If he's been into something, you'll have to give him a bath because you let him out. He must have found something to roll in, something decayed."

Pete groaned, irritation rolling off him in waves that smelled like a soured rag. "I'll get my coat."

I heard Pete leave the kitchen, clomping upstairs. I didn't wait. I opened the door and a blustery wind blew the hair away from my face. The back steps were covered with a thin, slick layer of snow. I noticed the open gate.

"Biscuit!" I yelled louder. Running through the gate, I looked right and left for him. No sign of the rascal. A larger dog would have had trouble hiding, but Biscuit could squeeze into small places, under brush, between gaps.

After running the perimeter of the house once, Pete stopped me. "Slow down."

"Yeah, yeah." I kept running and he followed. "Not with me. Go the other direction or we'll never find him."

"You stick close to the house. Biscuit will come back here. I'll look for him a little farther out."

"OK."

"You promise? Promise me."

"Sure. OK. I cross my heart." I drew my finger up and down, left and right over my chest. "Go. Get him."

"Bossy as ever." Pete ran to our gravel driveway that disappeared into thick woods before it met the main road. He jogged down the drive yelling Biscuit's name.

The wind cut through my fleece sweatshirt, through my pajama pants, through my bones.

I gritted my teeth to stop them from chattering, but it didn't help. Pete had been smart to get his coat. I turned to head back to the door when I saw a bit of Biscuit's fur sticking out from the front bushes lining the house.

Bounding over to him, I bent to the ground. I placed my hand on his back paw and he didn't budge.

"Biscuit, come on. It's colder than—" I suppressed a shivery seizure having nothing to do with the outside chill. Something felt darkly at odds, like an intuition, a premonition, my worst nightmare. I edged closer, holding my breath and angry that he had frightened me.

Biscuit's head rested half-hidden underneath a thick bush of red and gold leaves. Blood covered his ear and muzzle. I couldn't tear my focus away from his battered head.

Red, red, red, red.

I sank to my knees. A sharp pain knifed through my chest. Unforgiving branches scratched my face. I heard screaming that I didn't recognize. Screaming that seemed so far away.

My hands clung to his body.

"I'll take her into the house." I heard my dad's voice as though it was from miles away.

"Let go, Mia. Give Biscuit to me." I heard the sorrow in Pete's voice, but I didn't care.

"No, no, no," I screamed, attempting to cradle Biscuit's broken body. "No one is taking him!"

I hugged Biscuit, limp and cold, to my chest. I fought Pete as he pried my fingers away from the small, broken body.

A stabbing, monstrous grief burdened my soul.

* * *

"I'm fine. I want to be alone." I wanted to have a minute to think. To empty my brain of the burning image of the blood. I'd seen other things. Important things. Things that pointed to something other than a wild animal killing Biscuit. And I wasn't alone.

Pete's eyes had gone to the ground where a baseball bat lay under a bush near his foot. A baseball bat tinged in red. A baseball bat from our garage.

Pete looked at the garage and I did, too. For a split

second, I saw the green haze of hate and shock and fear envelope his body. I saw the footprints. Footprints in the snow.

Like footprints outside my bedroom window.

I looked at the limp, broken body in my hands and I knew. I knew that Dr. Eli Bleeker had killed Biscuit.

Knew hate like I hadn't known before.

Before...

"Sweetheart, did you hear me? I'm worried about you. Come down and eat some dinner." Dad hovered at my door. Worry weighed on each word like an invisible anvil.

"Please, Dad. I'm not hungry. I'll eat later." I stared at the bedroom wall, then forced myself to make eye contact. "I promise. Later."

Dad nodded once. A sad smile began at his mouth and stayed in his eyes. He slipped out the door and closed it behind him.

I didn't know where Pete went after. After my world fell apart. After the numb, red hate bled into my soul.

I unblocked Bleeker's phone number on my cell and waited.

The phone chimed once and the call confirmed what I knew in my heart.

I pressed the button. A lump formed in my throat and I wanted to spill my fury into his ear.

I could feel him on the line.

"Answering now, I see." Dr. Eli Bleeker's voice held a self-righteous edge.

"I am."

Hesitation weighed on the line. "I'm very sorry that it's come to such a tragic point in our relationship."

"We have no relationship." I needed to stay calm.

He tsked. "Mia. My work is important to me. I need a portal finder. You need to ensure the safety of those you love."

I began to shake and was glad he couldn't see me. I pressed my free hand to my mouth, smashing the sob back, breathing slowly.

"It will be difficult for me to do anything for you. Biscuit is..." I bit my bottom lip and tasted blood. *Breathe.* One thousand one. One thousand two. Steady. "...was very important to me." I would never forgive him for that. Ever.

"I understand. But I needed your attention. And now you understand the seriousness of this situation." His voice sounded regretful, but he was good at that. I pictured him, maybe sitting in a comfortable chair somewhere in those stupid suspenders he wore. Last fall, he'd fooled me with his earnest plea to help him get away from the IIA.

Biscuit had comforted me when Dad went away on work trips. When Pete left home without explanation. When Regulus broke my heart. And Biscuit always loved me, when I felt I had no one else.

"Mia, dogs can be replaced. It's much more difficult to replace people. I sent you photos earlier to prove how easily it could have been Regulus."

His words stabbed at my chest. Regulus's name on his lips placed a strangling grip around my throat. *Breathe.*

"What do you want from me?"

"I need portals found. I thought I'd made this clear. And you need to understand that I have a duty and I'll do whatever it takes to see it through."

Duty? What was he talking about?

"When?" I asked.

"You're agreeing?" He paused. "Good. Let's make the first meeting today."

"Fine. Where?"

"There is a water tower on Route 55. It's—"

"I know where it is. I'll be there in an hour." I needed an hour.

"Mia. You should come alone."

"Sure."

"Don't test me."

"I understand." I pressed END. Bleeker meant every word he'd said. And I intended to get him. I needed to see Bleeker's face when he realized that it was *game over*. After that, I'd let the IIA have him.

I dialed Arizona. His voicemail answered and I didn't leave a message. Bleeker had Regulus's phone so I couldn't call him.

I hit another number on speed dial. I had to hurry and count on getting away without Pete knowing. He would stop me and I knew what I had to do.

"Hey, Babe. Merry Christmas." Austin's voice soothed me.

"I need you to come get me. Help me."

There was a momentary pause. "Something wrong? You OK?"

"No. I'm not. Can you come?"

"I'll be there in ten minutes."

"Give me a little time. Be here in a half hour. And it's dangerous. You should know."

"Wouldn't expect it to be dull."

"Austin?"

"Yeah?"

"Thanks."

"Anytime, Babe. Anytime."

* * *

"Austin's coming over. I'll be outside talking with him. I want to tell him about Biscuit."

"Tell the boy to come in." Dad patted my shoulder and then tugged my earlobe, something he'd done since I was a kid. I stood in front of the window, my breath fogging up the glass.

"No, thanks. We like talking in the Jeep and listening to music. I need to get outside. "

Dad studied my eyes like a roadmap to my emotions. "It will hurt for a while, Sweetie. It'll get better." He pulled me into a quick hug.

"Where's Pete?"

"He went out to hunt for the coyote. Your brother's pretty broken up about it, too."

I could taste the bitterness in his voice.

"Good," I said.

"He wants you to stay inside. He's protective. Practically ordered me to keep you nearby." Dad shook his head. "I told him that I didn't expect you'd go anywhere."

"Well, he's here," I said. Austin gave a wave from the Jeep. "We might even take a drive. OK?"

Dad frowned and worry lines appeared on his forehead. "As long as the roads aren't slick. You'll need to be careful."

"Austin's Jeep has four-wheel drive. It'll be fine."

He mussed my hair. Outside, Austin bobbed his head in time as the stereo subwoofers drummed a bass beat through the windows. I ran down the porch steps and hopped in.

"You have trouble getting away? Your mom didn't care?"

"She's had so much spiked eggnog today that she doesn't care about much." Austin shoved his dark bangs out of his eyes and looked at his cell. "I'm on time. It's a first. Where are we going?"

"Water tower on Route 55."

"Gotcha. And why are we going there?"

"Bleeker. He killed Biscuit."

Austin stopped reversing the Jeep. "Come again?" His wide, startled gaze met mine.

"Yeah." I didn't want him to see the automatic tears that filled my eyes, so I looked away and stared at the bushes in front of my house. A dull ache rushed through my heart and pounded in my head.

"You're sure?"

"Yeah. Pete came in last night—"

"Pete's here?"

"Yes. He came in and told me that he needed to come home, that something was going down with Bleeker, that he was here to protect me, that—"

"Slow down." Austin put the Jeep in drive. "So, Pete's home. Where is he?"

"I'm sure he's hunting for Bleeker."

"And I take it Pete doesn't know that we're on our way to the psycho killer?"

I sighed. "Do you think he'd let me go?"

"Why don't you let him take care of this?"

"I'm not going to argue with you. I should have done the right thing a long time ago. I'm turning Bleeker in to the IIA."

"What about Regulus and Arizona?"

"Called Arizona. Got his voicemail." I told Austin about the photos sent by Bleeker from Regulus's phone.

"What's the plan?" He turned onto the highway.

"I have a stunner." I held up my phone. "I have handcuffs." The handcuffs made a jingling sound when I pulled them out of my purse and held them up.

"Nice." He winked at me. "I'm not even going to ask why you have those. I'm just going to imagine."

"Gross." I drew out the word.

"Can I borrow those sometime? You know...for crime fighting?"

Leave it to Austin to lighten the mood. "Snooped through Pete's bag to see if he had something I could use."

"Ah. I'll ask Pete."

I tried to smile. He was trying so hard. Like a visitor making casual conversation in the hospital cancer ward.

"I don't know how much control I have. I might kill him."

"With that?" Austin took his eyes from the road to examine my phone.

"Yeah. I've practiced with Regulus's stunner."

He pursed his lips and I wondered what he was thinking.

"Go ahead," I said. "Don't hold back."

The mountain road wound upward, a steep incline with curlicue curves. I winced at Austin's reckless driving. We were nearing the water tower.

"Stop the Jeep. I'm getting out here. He said I had to be alone." I rested my hand on the door handle.

Austin looked at me with lowered brows. "No way."

"I'm going to fling the door open. You'll risk me falling out."

"Mia, crazy talk." He shook his head frantically. "Stop. Hand off the door."

The key to bluffing is knowing how far to take it. The problem was that I wasn't bluffing. I was entirely prepared to open the door. He'd slow the Jeep. Probably.

"I'm jumping." He didn't slow down enough. "One." He grabbed my arm. "Two." I pulled the handle.

"Mia! Come on."

I took my hand away from the door. "Stop the Jeep and talk to me."

He pulled to the side of the road. "You've lost your ever-loving mind. I'm going with you. I don't know what you're thinking."

"Bleeker said I have to be alone. It's not going to work if you're with me."

Austin's eyes darted from me to the road. "What's he going to do? Shoot me?"

"Um...yes. I think he will."

"I said you're not going alone."

"Yes. We don't have time to argue. He's going to think I'm a no-show if I don't get out and run."

"Mia? What does Bleeker drive?"

"How would I know—"

"Don't turn around. Duck down in the seat. A Beemer is pulling up behind me. I'm going to pull out and leave."

I obeyed and rolled my body into a ball perched in the floor space. The Jeep surged forward and Austin accelerated at a speed that jolted my head against the glove compartment.

"What are you doing?" My voice was like a squeal.

"He's following us." The speedometer edging to forty.

"It's him? Bleeker?"

"Get up and put your seat belt on. He's right on my bumper. This dude has a death wish."

Chapter Nine

Afternoon Drive

Pete glanced at the passenger in his truck. Most people didn't understand Timothy "Tiny" McAlister. Tiny lived in a run-down farmhouse with his grandmother. A grandmother who doted on him with homemade fried pies and all the Internet service he required. He didn't attend college and he didn't work. He didn't date. Most people weren't sure what he did.

But Pete knew. He knew Tiny was busy programming and selling apps as quickly as he made them.

When he wasn't programming and playing the stock market like he belonged on Wall Street, Tiny played Quest of Zion. They'd discovered the game together and logged twenty-eight hours straight, playing until they'd collapsed from lack of sleep.

Operation Zodiac needed Tiny, but Tiny preferred to sit in his oversize computer chair and monitor the action from his computer. He didn't want to answer to anyone—especially the authorities.

"So what do you think about this Regulus guy?" Pete said.

"He's smart. Honest. Too honest if you ask me."

Pete smirked. "Too honest?"

"Been real honest with your sister. Girls don't always appreciate honesty. I mean, I'm honest, but I'm not trying to keep a girlfriend."

"He needs to concentrate on his duty and quit trying to hook up with my sister." Pete waited a few seconds, let his animosity take a backseat, then switched to a safe topic. "And you'd be honest— girlfriend or not. It's your nature."

Tiny grunted.

Pete gave a low laugh. "You and this Regulus guy may be more alike than you think."

"Regulus is not a bad guy."

"And Arizona? What about him?" Pete turned into the Whispering Woods University campus.

"He's a douche bag."

"Like him that much, huh?"

"I like him less than a remote access Trojan."

The computer virus reference meant Tiny seriously hated Arizona. He glanced sharply at his passenger before putting the truck in park. "Is there something I need to worry about with him?"

"No. It's Em that he's messing with—not Mia."

"I'm not worried about him asking my sister for a date. I'm interested in knowing if Arizona and Regulus can get Dr. Bleeker."

"Yeah, yeah." Tiny opened the truck door. "So, am I the good cop or the bad cop?"

Pete laughed. "Buddy, you just have to show me to their dorm room. Only been here once, a long time ago."

"Follow me."

* * *

Regulus and Arizona's dorm room had two beds, two desks, two closets, and enough room for two people. Three people currently stood in the room, including Pete. That's if Tiny counted as one.

Tiny sat at one of the desks as if he did it every day. The swivel chair appeared to be two sizes too small for him.

Pete waited for a second. Introductions must have been a foreign language to Tiny whose knowledge base consisted of computer languages.

"Hi. I'm Pete Taylor." He gave Arizona a nod. Then he looked around for a seat in the room. He'd seen closets larger than this.

"I'm Arizona. You're Mia's brother. The MIA brother."

"That would be me. Not really MIA, since I'm here." Obviously.

Arizona stared with curiosity. "You visiting?"

"I'm...working. I'm here to talk to you and Regulus."

"Regulus isn't here," Arizona said.

Pete nodded and checked his watch. Time was short and he needed to get back to the house.

"When will he be back?" Pete said.

"Pete asked me to bring him." Tiny looked at Arizona. "That crazy Dr. Bleeker killed Mia's dog. Hit him with a ball bat." Tiny shuddered.

Arizona winced. "Ah, man. How's Mia?"

"She'll be fine. But I'm more worried about her safety than I was earlier." Pete looked at Arizona. "I know you work for the IIA and they want Bleeker. Let's not play games. You know I work for OZ. We both want the same thing. It's stupid not to work together to stop this lunatic. Figure out how to take care of him."

Arizona nodded. "Go on."

Pete leaned on the edge of the desk and folded his arms. "We capture him together. The government wants him off US soil. You can take him in. It's a win-win."

"Agreed," Arizona said. "It might be easier if you joined the IIA. We can always use you."

Pete wanted to wipe the asinine grin off Arizona's face. He could see why Tiny wasn't a fan.

"Not gonna happen. Are you interested or not?"

"Interested." Arizona shrugged and gave him a friendly smile.

"What's this?" asked Tiny. He'd turned to the laptop and studied the highway map displaying a moving signal.

Arizona looked at Pete. "Your sister's on the move."

Pete grunted. "You're tracking my sister?" He stopped himself, calmed his voice, began again. "Does Mia know you're tracking her?"

"We've been worried that she'd get into trouble. The tracking chip is in the new phone Regulus gave her yesterday." Arizona gave a sheepish grin. "It was for her protection."

"I wondered why she had a pink phone. I bet she

hates that."

Arizona's eyebrows lifted. "She didn't say she hated it."

Pete chuckled. "Did she say she loved it?" He pulled out his phone. "Need to make a quick call. I asked my father to watch her. To keep her there."

"She's headed up the mountain." Tiny hunched over to point at the screen. "Highway 55."

"I need to know what she's doing out the house." Pete stepped to the door which only put two feet between himself and Arizona.

After making the call and tamping down the irritation that Mia couldn't stay put for a couple of hours, he decided he was lucky she'd left with Austin. Austin was trustworthy. It would look suspicious if he tried to trap his sister inside her room. He hoped Mia didn't guess that someone— most likely Bleeker—had killed Biscuit.

"And Regulus?" Pete waited a beat. "Let me guess. He's out there." Pete pointed at the screen.

"He left as soon as she did." Arizona sat on his bed.

"She's with Austin. Looks like they took a drive." Pete grabbed the remaining chair and sat. Looking out the window, he said, "Weather's getting worse. He'll take Mia back home."

Tiny kicked off his mud-caked hiking boots. "Mind if I see what else is around that area?" He didn't wait for Arizona to answer but proceeded to click and type. His fingers danced across the keyboard like a master pianist playing a concert, forgetting about the others in the room.

"Dude," Arizona said, "Can you leave those

puppies on?"

"Got 'em wet. My socks are wet, too." Tiny's monotone told them that he was not going to be distracted by any discussion of etiquette.

Arizona made a choking sound and muttered something about spray. He got up and opened the window.

Tiny leaned back in the chair, and Pete grimaced at the squeaking sound of metal and plastic stretched to the weight limit.

"Is this a front for your monitoring setup?" Tiny folded his arms over his chest and spun the chair in a circle and examined his surroundings.

"Huh?"

Tiny waved at the barbell and weights stacked in one corner. "This stuff. Is this here to make it look like you're a real college boy?" He picked up a graphing calculator from the desk.

Arizona snatched it from Tiny's hand. "Um, no. I use everything."

"So you really go to class here?" Tiny looked around the room. "I don't see any books."

Arizona leaned over and opened a metal cabinet mounted above the desk. It held stacks of books.

Tiny nodded. "Don't know how much of you is for real."

Arizona lifted one eyebrow. "I'm for real—whatever that means. Why the twenty questions?"

"Your buddy's already done a number on Mia and now you and Em—"

"They're going fast up the mountain. You need to quit worrying about Em and focus on this." Arizona pointed at the screen.

Tiny and Pete turned their attention to the screen and the fast-moving green dot.

"Dang." Tiny muttered the word to himself. He looked at Arizona. "They're flying. That road snakes up the mountain."

Pete stood and moved behind Tiny, watching the screen. "How close is Regulus?"

"Several miles. They've got a head start on him. He'll catch up. He's on his motorcycle," Arizona said.

Pete looked out the dorm window at the snow falling in heavy, wet clumps. Ice pinged against the window.

"Well, call Regulus. See what's up." Tiny pulled his knit cap off and rubbed his hand over his flattened red hair.

"He's hooked to that chip. He'll catch up to her in a minute," Arizona said.

Arizona's cell went off in a tiny pulsing beep. "Yes."

Pete looked away from the screen. He watched Arizona move to the window with the phone. Pete tried to listen to the one-sided conversation but Tiny's clicking on the keyboard distracted him.

"We see her, but we don't know why she's going so fast. She's with Austin," Arizona said.

The sound of clicking keys stopped. Pete glanced at the screen.

"Something's wrong," Tiny muttered.

"What'd you say?" Arizona asked.

"They're not on the road now." Tiny's voice went gruff. "They went off the highway."

Chapter Ten

Flying

The car slammed into us like a freight train, jerking me to the floor. I scrambled into the seat, grabbed the seat belt and attached it.

"I know he's crazy—" I fell forward and the shoulder harness caught me as the Jeep spun on the slick road. Bracing myself against the dash, I thought to tell Austin that he shouldn't slam on his brakes. I heard Dad's voice in my head, cautioning me the last time I'd driven in icy weather.

The vehicle spun and I saw a blur of trees and icicles. Austin wore a panicked expression and he kept turning the steering wheel, not able to stop us.

They say a person sees her life flash before her eyes during an accident.

I'd agree.

In those few seconds while I fought the need to scream, I wished that I'd told Austin that he and Em were my best friends and I loved them.

I prayed that my dad wouldn't be alone forever. He needed me.

I wanted Dr. Bleeker to pay for being the abominable man he was.

And I saw Regulus's face. A face I'd never see again. Regulus, who had no idea that my heart belonged to him.

We were off the road, over the side, down the embankment. My head yanked up and down from the force, an object slammed my chest, my right elbow popped against the passenger window.

A booming clap in my left ear took my breath away and I opened my eyes, not realizing that I'd closed them. I tried to move my arm, now wedged between Austin and his air bag.

Austin lifted his head from the driver's side window. "That asshole," he croaked. Strands of his dark hair stuck to a trickle of blood from his temple. A powdery substance stuck to his face.

I sucked in a lungful of air; it made me choke and cough.

"You're hurt." The pressure of my airbag decreased and it deflated away from my body. I tried to get up, but gravity and my seat belt trapped my body in the seat which slanted at an odd angle. A thousand cracks in the windshield obstructed my view.

"Hey." Austin rolled the word out in two syllables. "Don't move."

I rested my head against the seat.

Austin's calm voice continued. "Don't freak out when I say this." He waited a few seconds. "I think we're in a tree."

I squeezed my eyes shut and took a deep breath. "You're not making sense. Austin..." I opened my eyes and slowly turned my head to look at him. His head now rested at a tilt like he couldn't hold it up.

"We. Went over. The. Guardrail." A loud pop and the sound of creaking metal punctuated each of his last three words.

I sucked in a breath. A huge tree branch tunneled through the back and snaked to the left of Austin's head. It filled the rear seat of the vehicle.

The reality of our situation sent an electrifying jolt through me. The guardrail protected cars from a ravine at least six stories deep. I'd always sucked at calculating distance. I hoped I was overestimating.

"We have to get out."

"Right," Austin said with a hint of skepticism. "Listen, Mia. I think I'll stay here and rest. You're going to have to pull yourself out the passenger window. You can do this. When we were kids, you could climb a tree better than any guy I know."

I shifted in alarm to look at him. "We're both climbing out. You—"

The sound of the Jeep popping in the tree interrupted my train of thought.

"You're OK, aren't you?" I steadied the slight tremble in my words.

"I'm alive. I can't move. Pinned in." Austin gave the report matter-of-factly. He spoke evenly, like he might be talking about the new CD he'd bought.

Austin didn't move for several seconds. His breaths sounded shallow and thin.

Somewhere in the distance, I heard my name. The

urgent repetition of it stopped me from staring at Austin's unmoving form. "Here," I yelled. "We're here."

Another popping noise sounded from the side of the Jeep and the entire vehicle shuddered as if it were a beast waking from slumber. We tilted sideways.

"Mia. You need to go." Austin coughed. "Window." He brought one finger up to point at the passenger door.

"I'm not going without you."

"Don't be such a girl."

"I'm punching you for that. When we're both out—" A grinding noise stopped me from finishing. I unfastened my seat belt, reclined the seat away from the airbag, climbed upward and wedged one foot in the console with the other on the seat. I pushed upward to open the door, gravity fighting me all the way.

I attempted to stick my head out the open door and my sneakers slipped on the leather seat. The door slammed shut. My chin hit the edge of the seat. I tasted blood and heard Austin ordering me to get up.

I felt the sway of the seat and took a deep breath before pushing the door open again. This time, I noticed the open glove compartment and stuck my left foot into it. Bracing myself, I examined our location. When I looked down, I could see that I had been wrong when I'd estimated six stories. It had to be more. I gulped in air to steady my stomach.

A tree growing up the side of the mountain had stopped our descent.

"Mia. Don't move." The loud and demanding order didn't come from Austin. I looked up toward the voice.

Regulus stood at the top with something in his hands. I tried to figure out what he held when another pop of a tree branch slammed me back into the seat.

Something hit the windshield, forcing the glass inward. Shards of glass didn't fall onto my body as I'd expected. Instead, cracks formed small, uneven geometrical shapes in the window. Scooting off Austin, I pressed my hands into the glove compartment and pulled myself up again. Austin moaned.

At the new angle with my back against the dash, I saw the reason for Austin's inability to move. I broke into a sweat, shaking and unable to breathe. A branch had thrust through the back of the Jeep and impaled him, the tip of the broken wood peeked through his bloodied shoulder.

"Mia." The faint sound of Regulus's voice broke my trance.

"Yes," I called. A voice in my head yelled to move, but my body froze. I willed myself to stretch a couple of centimeters to the hand hold above the passenger door. My fingers shot out unsteadily to grab it. I could hear noises moving closer to the vehicle.

I used one foot to leverage myself against the console and pushed. With one hand pulling the door handle and my shoulder against the door, I pushed hard. The door rested on me as I used both hands to shove it upward like a submarine hatch. I peered up and out.

Regulus crouched at the edge of the road above. He made a stop motion with his hand. "No sudden movements. Are you hurt?"

"No," I yelled in a harsher voice than I'd intended.

He didn't answer for minute. Then he asked, "Do you see the cable I've sent down?"

I shook my head to clear the light-headed feeling that enveloped my foggy brain. The frigid air whipped my hair away from my face and pricked my ears.

"Look to your right." He signaled the direction and waited for me to obey before he continued. "Take the harness on the end. Put it around your waist and clip it. Check the clip."

"I'm not leaving him," I yelled. I pushed hair out of my eyes and glanced back at Austin. A drizzle of liquid ran onto my upper lip and I realized my nose was bleeding.

"No choice. Do what I tell you." He'd narrowed his eyes and shook his head. "You'll die if you don't put that around you." He paced along the top. "Do it," he yelled in an urgent voice.

I gritted my teeth. I heard the popping sound of wood breaking and the vehicle shuddered. Through Austin's window, I watched a branch fall.

I retreated with cat burglar grace inside my door. Gravity made the door feel like a lead weight. Austin's upper lip shone with a fine layer of perspiration. I blinked away traitorous tears. Crying was out of the question.

Inside the Jeep, Regulus's voice sounded very far away. I climbed into the backseat like a rock climber. No sudden fall to the back. Smooth and even.

Looking at the branch stuck through Austin's

seat, I felt my skin tingle with fear. I closed my eyes and listened to Regulus's directions that I should fasten the harness on my body.

Regulus muttered something unintelligible from above. I stuck my head back through a hole in the Jeep's soft shell. "What?"

"Fasten yourself and Austin. It should hold two."

"He's pinned to the seat," I said. "Tree branch." There was a panic in my voice that I struggled to control.

"Cut it." He waited for me to act. "Get your cell phone. The one I gave you. Use it to cut the wood."

It took me a minute to comprehend. I'd lived with the stunner for less than a day. I'd forgotten I could do that.

I scanned the topsy-turvy interior of the vehicle and my heart fell. Finding anything in the mess would be a miracle.

"Coat pocket," Austin breathed through almost blue-tinted lips.

I reached inside my pocket and grasped the cool object.

Austin lifted one corner of his upper lip. "Better move fast. I'm losing my ability..."

"Huh?" I held the phone in my right hand the way Regulus had shown me last fall.

"My ability to be charming." He finished and made steady eye contact with me. "Listen..."

"Shut up," I said and closed my eyes where I couldn't look at him. "I'm trying to remember how this works."

"That is exactly why you and I are only friends. Your bossiness is a total turn-off."

I opened my eyes to his smile. I shook my head to silence him.

Austin looked up toward the cliff we'd tumbled over to see Regulus. "He's loving this whole rescue thing. And he thinks you're a warrior or something."

"This is no time to talk." I maneuvered myself to the space where his shoulder was pinned.

"You and Em are my best friends. I need to tell you—" My words came out in a jumbled rush.

"And you talk too much, girl. I thought Em was bad, but—" Austin went another shade of pale when I pointed the cell phone with one hand and held his shoulder steady with my other hand.

I inhaled and focused my thoughts on operating the futuristic weapon. "Cut," I commanded.

Nothing.

The vehicle shuddered again and icy sleet began an onslaught on the metal. Pinging sounds coincided with Austin's two tiny whimpers.

"Ah, man. I hate rain," he said. "Unless I can go muddin'."

Once more I imagined seeing the invisible beam of whatever-made-this-thing work make a clean slice. This time, I didn't say a word. I saw it happen.

In amazing real-time accuracy with my imagery, the weapon sliced the branch.

Regulus's yelling echoed in my head. "Get the harness on you, Mia."

I tried lifting Austin to me. It took all my strength to pull him away from the seat. There was no way to get him out. I wasn't strong enough to even get the harness around him.

I looked up the cliff at Regulus. The sleet pelted

into my eyes, and I shielded them with my hand. "I can't get him. He's too heavy."

Even though Regulus was too far away for me to actually see his expression, I could sense the grimace.

"You first. I'll get him." Regulus screamed the words. I'd never heard him this frantic.

I sucked in my breath at another popping sound. A large branch fell past the front windshield. When I stuck my head out the passenger window, he yelled again.

"I promise." Regulus made a weird gesture that I'd never seen before. It meant something. Maybe an oath.

"You go or we're both going to die. Don't be stupid. I have a date Friday night." Austin grimaced again. "Hurry. Get your superhero down here to get me."

I shook my head and looked from Austin to the drop I could see past his window. "He's coming for you. I swear."

Austin winked. "Babe, I know." He winced, causing wrinkles around his eyes. "Go now. He's strong enough and you're not."

I stared at him for a second, pressing my trembling lips together.

"OK," I yelled to Regulus. I grabbed the harness and placed one leg through an opening. I wound the harness around my waist and secured the belt clip. Looking up, I couldn't see Regulus and was alarmed for a moment. He reappeared and stared at me.

"Ready?" He looked behind him again and turned back to me. "You'll be pulled up soon. Walk it."

I didn't know what he meant until the harness

pulled me and I fell against the side of the rock. The Jeep had tumbled down a steep hill, but the fall was at an angle. I grabbed the harness and moved my feet in front of me. The harness supported my weight and pulled me at the angle upward.

It was easier than I'd thought. At the top, Regulus grabbed my coat and hauled me to him.

He placed his face against the top of my wet hair and then pushed me away.

We heard a loud noise and saw that another segment of the massive tree holding the Jeep had cracked. The vehicle seemed to tip.

"I'm going down. You have to operate the winch." He led the way to his motorcycle farther up the highway. He'd secured it to a remaining segment of the metal highway guardrail. He pointed at a small control. "This button on the right starts and stops it. This knob on the opposite side has three positions: forward feeds the cable, center stops it, and back retracts it. It's running."

I didn't know how a winch had appeared on his motorcycle and I didn't question it.

"How will you get him?" My voice trembled.

"I think the winch will pull us both." Regulus already had the harness on and stood at the edge of the highway. Torn metal swayed where the Jeep had breached it.

"Don't you dare die." I knew my voice sounded angry. I'd been angry at him so much lately. But I couldn't lose him. Or Austin.

He raised one eyebrow, backed away and disappeared down the side of the mountain before I could continue. My fingers were numb and I walked stiffly to the edge. Regulus descended quickly, he was halfway down the embankment in seconds.

I could see a problem. The tree and the side of the mountain were not as close as I'd thought. Regulus might be a guy from another dimension, but he wasn't Superman. He couldn't fly over to the tree.

I blew hot air onto my hands to warm them. Sleet had stopped raining down on us for the moment. I rubbed my fingers to fight the numbness and noticed dried blood smeared across my knuckles. Something caught my attention in the periphery of vision. A vulture circling the treetops made a shudder dance along my shoulders.

Regulus perched with both feet on a ledge and leveled with the vehicle. His body wasn't close enough for a jump. He reached inside his coat pocket and swung his arm out from his body.

I couldn't see what he'd done, but I heard the clink of something hitting the metal of the Jeep. Although fear fingered along my spine,   I leaned over the edge to have a better view. Regulus had secured a line to the vehicle and was pulling his body across the gap.

Maybe not Superman, but he gave Spiderman some competition.

Regulus reached the Jeep and disappeared inside. I craned my neck to be able to see the progress.

I jumped at the sound of another ear-splitting pop. Standing outside the vehicle gave me an entirely different perspective. One I didn't want.

I couldn't prevent the squeal that escaped me.

A dark head of hair appeared for only seconds then disappeared. In the blinding snow, I imagined it was Austin's. I wiped snow from my lashes. That couldn't be right.

The motor pulling the rope and harness hummed softly. When I looked down at the Jeep wedged into the tree at the precarious angle, I blinked hard.

Austin's body swung out across the divide on the pulley system that Regulus had devised. With the harness secured, Austin wore a makeshift sling wound from his shoulder to the opposite side of his waist. The arrow-like tree branch that had spiked through his shoulder no longer appeared at his front. A dark red flower of blood decorated the sling.

The motor pulling the harness up the ravine operated at a devastating rate of slowness. On the one hand, it was hard to be upset about the speed of the device that'd saved our lives. On the other, I could crawl to Alaska faster than the harness moved.

The temperature outside made the landscape a frigid wasteland. I hopped from foot to foot, frenzied and freezing by the time I could grab the harness at Austin's waist. He grunted lowly when I pulled him to the ground to undo it. I needed to get him out of it. Fast.

Austin attempted to help, but his fingers worked like he wore gloves. I brushed his fumbling aside.

"I've got it." I unfastened the clasps holding the apparatus around him. I maneuvered his knee, pulling the straps away from his body. He yelped.

"OK, OK, OK," I mumbled, each word rising in tone and volume. I continued to remove straps. "I'm not trying to hurt you. I need to send this back."

I ran over to the winch on the motorcycle and saw smoke rising from area below the knob. Forward to send the cable out. Toward me to retract. I dialed the knob forward and nothing happened. I twisted it back and forward again. Nothing again.

I felt dizzy when I realized that Regulus wasn't coming back up in the harness. I dropped into a crouch, put my elbows on my knees and tried to stop shaking.

Chapter Eleven

Suspension

"Regulus told me to tell you that he was sorry. He's sorry he hurt you and..." Austin rubbed his face. "...and sorry that he pushes you to do things you don't want. He said—"

"Shut up!" I screamed into his face. If I listened, I acknowledged the fact that he could die. "He can get his butt up here and tell me himself." One more word and I was going need a straightjacket. "Please, give me a minute. I'm thinking," I said, softening my voice from its previous bullhorn level.

My breakdown was interrupted by the sound of Regulus calling my name. I looked to the tree that appeared more splintered than five seconds ago. Had I missed that tell-tale sound?

I ran to the shoulder of the road where we'd gone over the side. "The winch is broken." My voice came out high and panicked.

"Call Arizona," Regulus bellowed at me.

I felt stupid for not thinking of that before. My scratchy throat ached and each beat of my heart pounded in my head. It would've been nice if the two people *not* in danger could think straight.

Arizona answered at one ring. "We're almost there. What's happened? My monitoring system says Regulus is off-road."

Regulus's implanted GPS chip did occasionally come in handy. Handy or not, it gave me the creeps thinking about being tracked twenty-four seven.

"Regulus needs you now. He's about to fall from a Jeep stuck in a tree." My explanation sounded straight from the pages of a Marvel comic, but Arizona didn't question it.

"Is he injured?" Arizona sounded calm.

"No." I cringed at the vision I had of the vehicle falling into the ravine and bursting into flames. I looked up to see Tiny's old truck spinning around the corner of the highway and nearly slamming into Regulus's motorcycle.

A black truck appeared behind it.

Two people leaped out of Tiny's truck. Arizona did a half glide, half run to meet me while Tiny took tentative scooting steps to avoid falling on the sheet of ice.

Pete emerged from the second vehicle and followed right behind them. What was he doing here?

"Sis. You all right?" Pete grabbed my upper arms.

"Yeah." I exhaled and shivered. "Somebody help Regulus. Hurry."

I grabbed Pete's arm harder than I intended. "Do something. Please."

"I've got this." Arizona wasn't looking at me but at the mangled Jeep. He had a backpack that I hadn't noticed. He unzipped the bag and removed something that resembled a handheld cannon.

"No books in the backpack, huh." Tiny peered into the bag to see the other contents.

"Hey Pete. It's about time you showed," Austin said from his position on the ground. "Long time no see. When you leave home, you *leave* home."

Pete's disappearance that had been so traumatic to me had also affected so many others. Sometimes, I forgot about his friends and how they'd been affected.

Pete quickly lifted his chin in the man-nod. "Good to see you. You could take better care of my sister though. What happened to your shoulder?" Pete grimaced.

"Little scratch," Austin ground out.

Why was it so hard for a guy to admit he's hurt?

"Lot of blood for a scratch." Pete raised both eyebrows and bent, moving closer to Austin's shoulder.

"Hey, hands off." Austin shooed Pete's incoming hand.

"Humph. You can't be too hurt," Pete said.

Austin grunted. "This body can take a lot. Plus dude rubbed something on it. Stopped the bleeding. You decide to come home for good?"

"Can you two catch up later?" Arizona held the cylinder on his shoulder and squinted through a hole at the end.

I shrieked and lunged for the weapon. "You're going to shoot him? You're crazy." I attempted to wrestle it out of Arizona's hands. The slippery ground beneath us made it difficult to keep my balance.

"A little help here," Arizona said to Pete. "I'm not shooting him."

To my surprise, Pete obeyed and snaked one arm around my neck and pulled me to his chest.

Arizona ignored my screaming, aimed and pushed a series of buttons on the side of the gun to fire.

A net sprang from something within the shot. It hung suspended in air at an angle from the Jeep, draping from vehicle all the way to the ground like a fireman's safety net. The material appeared as translucent as ice with only hints of existence.

"It looks like a giant slide. What's holding that?" I marveled breathlessly.

"Quantum levitation," Arizona said. He carefully placed the cylinder on the ground. "I picked the shape and location and it works like a magnet to—" He looked at my face. "Didn't need to know that much, huh?"

"Um...that answers everything and nothing. Is it going to bring him over here?"

"I need one of those," Austin quipped from his sitting position on the ground. "It can be the mini version. I'm not picky."

Pete loosened his hold on me.

"Sorry for not trusting you," I turned to Arizona. "I should have known you wouldn't do anything to hurt him."

Tiny put a hand on my shoulder. "Everything's going to be OK."

I put my free hand over his, and he quickly yanked

his away. Warm and fuzzy time was over.

"So now what?" I glanced over to see what Arizona planned to do next.

Arizona stood with one hand over his mouth in a musing pose. "Don't know yet."

Three heads pivoted in his direction. He never lost focus but continued to look at the problem in front of him. "I can't think with people looking at me."

For once, Arizona didn't look smug and carefree. His brow was furrowed and he rubbed his upper lip with his index finger.

I turned to Austin and squatted next to him. "You still making it?"

"Yeah," he said.

"Arizona?" Regulus yelled from the Jeep.

He didn't poke his head out, but I recognized that commanding, bossy voice. I was glad to hear it. He could yell at me anytime. Just as long as he made it out alive.

"Working on it," shouted Arizona. He rummaged in the backpack.

"Got an aspirin in there?" Austin looked up at Arizona. I noticed for the first time that he was covered in snow. We all were. In another half hour, we'd look like snowmen. Or we'd lose limbs from frostbite.

"Can someone get Austin into some heat while you're thinking?" I asked.

Tiny held up his truck keys. He placed them in my palm and I examined the ring that held over ten keys, a bottle opener and a rabbit's foot. Tiny grabbed them again and handed the key ring back with one key extended. He bent and placed an arm around

Austin to pull him to a standing position.

I heard a muffled groan and saw Austin gritting his teeth in pain.

"Maybe you should carry him," I suggested.

Tiny gave me a look. "You have a screwy sense of humor." He walked with Austin to the truck. The two quickly glided over the ice, with Tiny moving like a graceful giant.

I pivoted back to Arizona. He still wore the same concerned expression.

"I've created a way for him to get out of that Jeep and onto the ground," Arizona said. "We need to get him up here."

* * *

"He can't walk up the side of an icy mountain. He might be able to climb, but it's easier going down a cliff than up." Pete gave me the big-brother eye roll.

"We could send a rope over." Tiny sounded sincere or I'd have thought it was a joke.

"Go on." Arizona seemed intrigued.

"I have a compound bow. And rope. I can attach rope at the end and shoot down to him." Tiny narrowed his eyes, looking at the wreckage. "I need to know my target and if he'll use the rope to pull himself up to us."

Tiny darted off to retrieve the gear. After quickly tying off the rope on one end of the arrow and handing Arizona the other, Tiny lifted the bow to aim.

"Wait," Arizona said. "What if the distance is farther than you think and I'm holding the end?"

"You'll be jerked off the side of this mountain."

Tiny kept the same serious expression. "But it's not."

"Perfect. Do it," Arizona replied. His wide eyes gave me the feeling he wasn't sure, but he was willing to take the risk.

Tiny shot the arrow in one fluid motion that was over before I even saw him draw back. I couldn't do anything but gape when the arrow hit a tree trunk midway between us and the Jeep at a point of sharp incline.

A loud pop from the tree holding the Jeep took my breath away. Liquid drizzled from the bottom of the vehicle.

"Get out," I screamed. The net acting as a slide for Regulus billowed out in a wave. Regulus popped up from the door.

I watched in horror as Regulus maneuvered himself to the top and executed a freefall down the nearly invisible netting to the ground.

A second later, the Jeep shimmied down the splitting tree and rolled down the steep mountainside until hitting the boulder that stopped it.

The vehicle lay upside down on the incline and smoke roiled from the engine.

Regulus walked to the arrow stuck in the tree and cut the rope from it.

"Those arrows aren't cheap," Tiny said.

"I'll get you another," answered Arizona. He gave an unflattering snort and shook his head. "Priorities, man, priorities."

Regulus attached the rope to himself and lifted one hand to signal Arizona.

Tiny and Arizona reached out to pull Regulus to

the top of the mountain.

I threw my arms around him. "You're OK. You scared me. You—" And then I realized what I'd done and pulled my arms away.

I took two steps back and a rush of blood warmed my face. Pete stared from me to Regulus and back.

"Oh. Regulus, this is my brother, Pete. Pete—"

My cell phone rang.

I interrupted the awkward 'this is my other dimension ex-boyfriend to my super secret agent brother intro' and studied my phone's display. "It's Bleeker."

Pete attempted to take the phone from me and Regulus held up a hand. "We should hear what he wants. Speaker phone, OK?" Regulus edged closer and I found myself wedged between my brother and Regulus.

I answered. "Hello." I pressed SPEAKER and held the phone out.

"I thought I told you not to bring anyone." Bleeker didn't sound angry. That concerned me.

"I needed a ride," I answered. "You almost killed me. How am I going to help you if I'm dead?"

"Do you think I'm stupid? You're playing a dangerous game, Mia. I only wanted to make a point. I'd have shot you if I wanted you to kill you."

Suspicion boiled to the surface in a rush. "How did you know I would answer? I could be dead. We went over."

Bleeker laughed. "I watched to be sure. I do need you around. Thought I'd have to save you myself. That would be ironic, wouldn't it?" He gave a soft chuckle. It was warm and relaxed and made me want to scream.

"Mia. I want you to listen to me closely. I truly regret that losing your dog didn't make you understand. Maybe losing a parent will. You'll do what I say."

Icy fear scraped my spine. I began shaking again. Regulus reached out to steady my unsteady hand. My entire body shook as I pressed END. My brain seemed to be shutting down. Pete ran, his boots pounding on the road, unwavering on the ice.

He stopped for a brief instance with his hand on the door. "You've got her?" He pointed at me.

I needed Pete to stop. To stay with me. To be safe.

"I won't leave her side." Regulus stared at Pete.

I realized why Pete was leaving without me. He was going to Dad. I couldn't do anything more than stare at his taillights with my teeth clattering together.

"We've got this." Tiny looked at me. "Get in the truck. Take care of Austin."

"Yes," Arizona added. "There's a medical case in my backpack. Take a blue square and place it in his mouth."

I opened my mouth to argue, but I understood that Austin needed me.

I bent obediently to rummage through the backpack. I'd been with him another time when Regulus needed medical attention. They used drugs in their world that were superior to ours.

There were lots of things in the pack, but I didn't spot a medical case. I turned objects over looking for the Red Cross symbol.

"It's not here."

"Oh. Sorry. It's that case that has that the *Muse*

sticker. Looks like a CD case." He pointed. "There. You're missing it."

I cocked my head up to glare out him. "Who puts a first aid kit in one of these?" The hard plastic case looked like it would hold a collection of CDs.

"I don't have CDs but I liked the case," he said.

"Who listens to *Muse*?" mocked Tiny, not taking his eyes off Regulus.

We both ignored Tiny. I removed the case from the pack and walked to the truck in a skating motion. I commanded my fingers to cooperate as I struggled with the latch of the old truck.

I climbed in and edged over to sit next to Austin. He peered sideways at me, his head resting against the seat.

"You OK?" he asked me.

"I'm fine. Bruises maybe." I lifted the makeshift bandage. "Don't move."

My hands, ears, and nose tingled as the warmth of the heater blowing at full blast thawed my body. Arizona's case held only a few items and I understood now why he'd instructed to use the blue square. The flat papery square couldn't be missed. There were dozens of them in the container. Nothing else.

"Open up." I held one in the air before his mouth. "Arizona said to give you this."

"You crazy? No. Not taking that."

"Trust me. Do you think I'd give you something that I wasn't a hundred percent sure about?"

Austin closed his eyes for a minute. "Regulus already did something to me in the Jeep. He made the bleeding stop. I'm fine."

"You are stubborn and surly and—"

He reached across the seat to touch my knee. "Shut up and give it to me." He opened his mouth.

I placed the blue square underneath his tongue as I'd seen Arizona do for Regulus once. Austin sighed and closed his mouth. I flexed my numb fingers as I waited for the medicine to take effect.

Austin grinned.

"You're good?" I took in the delirious expression on his face.

"Better than good. Can I have another?"

"Um..." I attempted to look out the truck window but our breaths and the heat had fogged up the windows.

"I'm kidding with you." Austin laughed at my indecision. "Those are some good drugs. You should stash a few in your pocket for later."

I shook my head to let him know that wasn't happening. "Did it numb you?"

"No. I feel great." He looked at his shoulder underneath the cloth we'd wound around him to cover the wound. "It's like a magic Harry Potter spell."

"Huh?"

"Look," he said and pushed the makeshift sling and bandage aside. "Does this look like normal recovery?" He did a little head dance from side-to-side.

"Whoa." It was the only thing I could say. "Amazing." I smiled at his boyish glee. Then my smile froze when I thought about Pete and Dad.

I was so tired of wanting to cry all the time. After Biscuit's death, I'd practically cried myself dry.

"Give me a hug. We didn't die." He grabbed me to his previously wounded shoulder and pulled me in tight.

The door opened at that moment.

I turned my head in surprise and saw Regulus jerk his attention from us to a point above the truck.

"I didn't mean to interrupt." Regulus looked at Austin and not me when he said it. "I need the blue."

I stared at him, uncomprehending.

Regulus straightened and pointed at the CD holder in my lap.

"Blue?" My voice came out high-pitched and nervous and stressed. My world was falling apart. I handed him the box when he continued to point at the Muse sticker-covered plastic case.

"What else would one call it?" he asked.

I stared at him numbly.

"I have a superficial cut. I'll shut the door. Sorry," Regulus said.

He slammed the door and the truck shook. I jumped at the suddenness and frowned.

"You should give him a second chance," Austin said.

"I am not talking about this with you. Are you crazy? All he wants is his portal finder. Nothing else. I'm tired of these games. And remember, he's the one who broke it off with me. Not the other way around. He forgot me. Forgot everything we had, Austin. And he thinks the IIA had the right to do it. Because he's following their rules. Always. Do you know how that feels? No? Right."

I sniffled into the silence as my nose began to run in the heated interior of the truck. I would not look at him.

"You're an idiot. He didn't forget you. He was brainwashed, so you can't blame him for that." He waited a beat. "He's miserable. You're miserable. What's the point of that." He said as a statement rather than a question. "If you are trying to punish him, it's working."

I wanted to slap him. "I can't believe you said that. I'm not like that. You act like I'm doing something vindictive and...and...I'm not."

"You're acting like a scared little girl. I thought you had more guts than that. I thought—"

"I don't need the guilt trip." My voice rose and I couldn't seem to stop it. "We start seeing each other again and then the IIA decides they'll pull the old mind wipe trick and I have to suck it up all over again. I'm not doing it. I won't be—"

A sharp rap at the window stopped me.

The door opened, and Regulus stuck his head inside. "We need to leave. You finished in here?"

Regulus asked the question like Austin and I had been making out and not arguing for the last few minutes. I glared at him with a fragment of leftover emotion.

"Thanks, man. I think you saved my life tonight," Austin said. "I owe you."

"No."

"Yeah, you did. And that stuff you said to me back there? It's a non issue. I'm stepping back. Mia's yours."

I shoved Austin's arm without thinking and he paled.

One side of Austin's mouth tipped up. He ignored

me and held out a hand.

Regulus looked at Austin's hand for a long moment before moving into the handshake. The gesture was over in seconds but seemed to signal a new phase in their relationship. I ignored them both.

"Excuse me." I slid across the seat and forced Regulus to move aside. My body ached. Nothing really hurt earlier in the cold when I thought I might die. Now, I felt everything, from my toes to my taste buds. I moaned when I stepped out of the truck.

"Hey." I came up behind Tiny and Arizona and looked over the edge. The Jeep hadn't exploded or any of those other things I'd imagined from the movies. It smoldered.

"Austin OK?" asked Arizona.

"Very OK. Lucky to be alive."

"How did you go over?" Arizona scratched his head.

Tiny glanced at the shorn piece of metal that had once protected vehicles from the steep edge. "I've lived here my entire life. No one's ever gone over the highway safety barriers. At least, I don't remember it ever happening."

"Bleeker," I said. One word. No explanation necessary for the name synonymous with evil.

Chapter Twelve

Bad to Worse

I looked out over the valley to see that we'd lost daylight. The roads grew more dangerous by the minute. Arizona and Regulus finished whatever they'd done to conceal their activity. The motorcycle sat against the side of the limestone cliff.

My own cell rang. 'Dad' appeared in the lit screen.

"Mia, where are you?" Dad's voice held an angry, anxious tone.

"Dad, we had a wreck but I'm OK and—"

"Where? I'm coming now," he answered like he wanted to reach through the phone and strangle me.

"Dad, calm down. I said I'm fine. I'm at the top of Dagger Mountain. The ice is bad. I don't know if you can make it here. Is Pete at home yet?"

"I'm on my way. Don't leave."

He hung up on me, and I stood staring at the phone.

I turned to realize I had an audience. The guys circled me and must have been there throughout the call. I stared at my phone, wishing I had Pete's cell phone number.

"Tiny's truck ran out of gas. We need everybody in the cab before the warmth is gone," Regulus ordered.

One girl and three guys couldn't fit into the cab of a truck. Tiny alone was the size of an NFL linebacker. Regulus had lost his mind.

Tiny the Jolly Green Giant. That's what we called him after failing to squeeze everyone into the cab of the truck. I texted Dad that we also needed gas. Austin called the police to let them know about the accident and that a tow truck couldn't get to his vehicle. He failed to tell them it was now a mess of metal lodged at the bottom of the ravine among brush and trees.

We drew straws for sitting inside the truck cab. I suspected that Tiny had rigged his fate as he organized the lottery and drew the short piece of grass. Outside in the bed of the truck, he covered up with a blanket. He said he kept it for napping sometimes. Strange, but handy.

A policeman and my dad arrived within minutes of one another. The blood and lack of any real injuries had been difficult to explain. After Austin answered questions for the officer's report, we had permission to leave.

We piled into Dad's Suburban. "Did Pete find you?" I sat in the front and stuck my stiff fingers against heat vents on the dash.

Dad gave me a funny look—sad and curious at the same time. "I saw him briefly. He's at the house."

"Why didn't he come with you?"

"Let's talk after I get the boys home." Dad white knuckled the steering wheel and stared straight ahead.

As we approached the road a mile from our house, a tow truck pulled out with a car on the back, smashed into an accordion.

Dad glanced at me. "I heard about this wreck before I called you." He nodded at the leaving tow truck. Sheriff Alder called me about it.

"Oh. I guess that got you worried. Dad, I'm fine. It scared me and I'm banged up, but nothing serious. Who had the wreck?"

He didn't answer but stared ahead. We'd started down our driveway. The heavy weight of the Suburban kept us steady on the ice. The darkness pressed in and the headlights illuminated a new torrent of sleet.

I didn't ask again.

Dad and I entered the house and Pete gave me a quick nod. "I'm glad you're home."

I quizzed him with my eyes. A strange vibe emanated from Pete, a brown haze of irritation—or maybe it was exhaustion—enveloping his entire body.

"Can I talk to you?" I asked Pete.

"Not now, Sis. Need to make a call."

Pete turned to Dad. "Have you talked to her?"

OK. This had to be about me leaving the house. And how had Pete even known where to find me?

Dad shook his head. Pete pivoted and walked to the kitchen without another word.

"I'm going upstairs. I'm so tired." I put one foot on

the stairs and waited for him to tell me no. To lecture about the trouble I'd gotten into lately.

He didn't stop me.

Five minutes later, he knocked on my door and poked his head through the opening.

"Mia, can I come in?" His voice wasn't angry like it had been on the phone. He sounded hesitant. Uncertain.

I sat up in bed. "Dad, you have to stop worrying. It was like a freak occurrence that I've been in two wrecks in the same year. I try to be safe. You know me." I knew he was thinking about the wreck I'd had in the fall that put me in the hospital.

He held up his hand in the universal language for stop. "Mia." Settling on the edge of my unmade bed, he put his face in his hands for a moment. I hated that I'd worried him so much.

"What Dad? What's wrong?" I hadn't seen him like this in a long time. "What was Pete talking about downstairs? I—"

"Something terrible has happened." Dad waited. "This entire town will be talking about it soon."

I frowned. I couldn't imagine anything that he could tell me that could be that bad.

"I'll come out and say it. I don't know another way." He developed a concentrated fascination with the crease in his jeans.

We sat in silence again.

"You're pregnant," I said to break the silence.

He didn't laugh. "Your mother has called several times in an effort to reconnect with you."

"So? I don't want that. Tell her no." I didn't know what Nancy wanted. Nor did I care. Most likely, she wanted to see my untimely death over the side of a mountain.

Since Dad had no knowledge of my secret double life this year, I stopped myself from sharing those thoughts.

"No. You won't be talking with her." He looked again at my walls.

I waited.

"The call I had earlier from Sheriff Alder. It was about that wreck. Something terrible has happened to your mother. Nancy was in that wreck. She hit a culvert and flipped the car. She died instantly."

"Oh." I was stunned. "She's dead?" As soon as I asked the stupid question, I shook my head at it. I was having a hard time grasping the concept.

Dad tilted his head to one side as if thinking. "I should have let you meet with her. I should have told you about her phone calls. She was obviously coming here. I should have..." He paused, looking like he might cry.

My throat pinched and I took a few deep breaths in and out and in to coax it into relaxing. I would not cry. I would *not* cry. If I cried, he'd think it was for her. I'd never cry for her. Growing up I'd watched my older brother Pete cry too many times after he asked if she'd called or if she would come home.

"I took away that chance because I didn't want you to get hurt."

"Is Pete all right?" I asked. The steadiness of my voice surprised me.

He nodded. "He's taking it better than I thought. He arrived when the ambulance did. Sheriff Alder knew it was Nancy. Recognized her."

"Oh." What was wrong with me that I couldn't say anything else?

The pressure in my head had nothing to do with grief over her. I didn't know her. Really, I didn't. My life was out of control. First, I lost Pete to an undercover agency, then Regulus to the IIA. And Bleeker had taken Biscuit from me.

Did Dr. Bleeker kill Nancy? Who would he kill next?

My chest filled with rage, a black poison moving up my throat to choke me.

Dad jumped up from the bed and appeared at my side. "Sweetheart. I'm so sorry." He pulled me up into a hug.

I let him. He rubbed his hand over the top of my head. His tenderness made me want to cry but my eyes were sandpapery dry. I wiggled out of his arms.

"I'm fine. Really fine." I closed my eyes. "Can I have some time alone, Dad? Are you OK?"

"Yes," he said, raking both hands through his hair. "It was a shock. I don't think it's sunk in. I'm worried about Pete. I don't think it's real to him. He was so close to your mother before she left. You may not remember—"

"Dad. Can you..." I looked at the door.

"Sure." He backed away. "I think you need some rest from that wreck. You could have been killed. And now this bad news after Bis—" He took a deep breath. "Take a nap. Rest."

I watched the emotions cross his face.

"I will. Thanks."

He walked stiffly to the doorway before turning. "Everything will be fine. We'll get past this. I'll talk to you later about the funeral."

I hadn't even thought about that detail. I flung myself across the bed and buried my head under a pillow. I thought I heard a scratching and for one brief second, I rose to open the door for Biscuit. I realized my own stupidity. My dog was gone. That woman was gone.

I told myself to calm down and rationalize. Everything required some action from me, and I couldn't stand the pressure.

* * *

Dad opened my door. "Mia? Didn't you hear me?"

I moved the pillows aside. "I thought you told me to take a nap." I leaned my head on the door frame.

"Regulus is downstairs."

I frowned at him. "Why? What does he want?" I gulped and hoped Dad couldn't hear what sounded abnormally loud in my head.

"I told him that you didn't want company. He started quizzing me about how you were feeling after the wreck." Dad's gentle voice edged on apologetic.

"Mia?" Regulus said from somewhere too close.

Dad jerked his head around. "Son, I told you I'd come and get you if she—"

Regulus stood at the top of the stairs and a few feet away from my door. I could see his narrowed eyes full of determination. I'd seen that expression enough to know he wasn't giving up easily.

"I need to talk to you." Regulus completely ignored my dad, and it was the first show of disrespect I'd ever seen him display.

"You need to turn around and leave." The threat in Dad's voice alerted me to the explosiveness of the situation. He stepped in front of me and consequently blocked the view.

"Dad." I put my hand on his shoulder. When he didn't respond, I gave him a squeeze. "I'll talk to him."

Dad turned his head and whispered as if Regulus didn't stand within hearing distance. "I'll escort him to the door if you say the word."

"No...no. It's fine." I attempted to make myself sound light and unburdened. "He'll only stay for a few minutes."

Dad stood a second longer than necessary in a show of fatherly protection. Then he sighed and stepped aside. He didn't look at Regulus again. I think he was torn between being worried about me and angry at Regulus for intruding.

I watched Dad walk down the stairs before I turned to Regulus.

Regulus took two steps and stopped. "Are you upset?"

"Not really." I answered in a raspy tone lacking enthusiasm. I was, but he didn't have to know it. My body ached from the wreck and pain reliever tablets hadn't helped. My brain protested from trying not to think about Nancy. I'd never have my answers about her. I wouldn't know if she'd regretted leaving me.

"Can I come in?" He invaded the personal space boundaries I'd erected since our breaking up by not waiting for an answer. I stepped aside rather than let our bodies touch as he entered my bedroom.

I folded my arms across my chest and stared

blankly across the room. "I told you I'm fine. I need to rest. That's all." I knew he was staring at me in that dissecting way he had.

"I know about what happened to your mother."

"How?" I focused on him. "That was quick."

"Pete sent me a message. I called Em. She brought me. She's downstairs."

"Wow. Huh." I seemed incapable of full sentences.

Regulus had been awkward when I'd first met him in the fall. Some might call him stand-offish. He didn't seem either as he moved closer to me.

I danced back a step and my legs touched the bed.

"You are not fine. I understand that this is a shock and you're distraught." He nodded his head like he wanted me to agree.

"Don't tell me what I am. I didn't know her."

He ran a hand over the back of his neck and looked away. "I want to help. Arizona told me about Biscuit."

I flinched.

"And now this."

"You've helped enough. When you first came to Whispering Woods, you promised to help with finding my brother. He's been found. We're done."

"You are part of my team," he said. "I am responsible for making sure you're OK." His referral to my role as a gatekeeper was the wrong thing to say to me. Guarding the security of portals near my home didn't interest me much anymore. I did want Dr. Bleeker stopped. He'd killed Biscuit. Maybe I could do this with Pete. But I didn't need Regulus.

"So, why did Pete tell you about Nancy? You guys just met." I sat on my bed.

Regulus grabbed the chair from my desk and sat at a good distance from me. I took a deep breath and tried to relax. My chest hurt from the effort.

"He thinks Bleeker was involved."

"No. She had a wreck. People have wrecks. Austin and I..." I studied the pattern of the comforter on my bed. Tracing the stitching with my finger, I let the thoughts trickle down like an unpleasant drip into my brain. I stopped when I noticed my hand shaking. *Breathe in. Breathe out.*

"Bleeker threatened you with the loss of a parent. He didn't say which one." Regulus leaned in until I could see his head near mine.

I closed my eyes. One more deep breath. I opened them. "I think I'm going be sick."

Leaving the room without a backward glance, I stumbled into the bathroom and made it to the toilet before expelling clear liquid that burned my throat.

In a detached way, I remembered that I hadn't eaten in a while.

"Mia, open the door."

"Go. A...way," I said before heaving again.

A pair of hands pulled my hair out of my mouth and face. When I'd stopped, he leaned me back to rest against him. "I'm here," he said in a near whisper. "Don't move."

I wedged my forehead into the space between my knees and mumbled protests at the hands that attempted to lift my head.

Regulus placed at wet cloth against my face. "I'll be back."

Dad returned with him. I sensed that familiar presence at my side and leaned my head against his shoulder when he placed a gentle arm around me. They whispered above my head and Dad helped me to my feet.

After taking me to my room, Dad said, "Lie down. Regulus is bringing you some ice chips."

"I need to brush my teeth." I gave an unhappy moan. "I'm not going to throw—"

I dry-heaved for a moment with Dad scrambling to get the trashcan underneath my head. Afterward, I lay back while mumbling, "Never mind..."

I heard voices and realized that now Em was in my house to witness my mortifying vomit session. This had to be one of the top ten worst days of my life.

"Is she all right? What can I do?" Em's voice was low, but I could hear her. Regulus answered even lower and I couldn't hear him. Dad's answer was lost as well.

"Hey you," Em said.

I nodded without opening my eyes. "What do you want? I can't talk right now."

"Oh, Mia. I'm so sorry. Sorry your life is such a suckfest right now." For some reason, her gentle female voice and her hand on the top of my head was my undoing. A hot tear traveled down my face. Yes, mortifying would totally describe this day.

Em's body forced the mattress to dip in the middle of the bed. She curled up behind me and placed an arm around me.

"I want my dog back. I could deal with everything if I had Biscuit. He always made things better." I squeezed my eyes shut against the world.

"I know." She rubbed my arm. "I know."

* * *

When I woke, I panicked in a disoriented way that only happens when you've been in a deep sleep.

"What are you doing here?" I attempted to scoot back to the headboard.

Regulus sat on my bed and dropped a book to the floor. Looking guilty, he retrieved it and left my room without a word. He returned with Em.

"You're still here." I sat incredulous and confused and stared at her. Then I remembered that she'd brought Regulus to my house and he wasn't gone either. "Both of you." I lay back and closed my eyes, hoping they would disappear like a bad dream.

"Mia, I wanted to stay and help. Let's get you cleaned up," Em said.

"Why cleaned up?" My words came out slow and suspicious.

"You have a little vomit on you." She waited for argument. Encouraged by my silence, she continued, "A lot of vomit."

"I can clean myself up. I've been doing it since I was a toddler."

"Yeah. Sure. But your dad asked me to stay. He doesn't want you in the bathroom alone. It's either me, your dad, or Regulus."

We had a momentary stare-down.

"Well, when you give me such stellar choices..." I mumbled as sat up. "I'm a little dizzy."

"Uh-huh," she answered. "When's the last time you ate?"

"I don't know." Mumbling seemed to be my new mode of communication.

Em took my elbow and guided me to the bathroom. I took one look in the mirror and moaned.

"What's wrong with my hair?"

"Well...if it wasn't there before, it might be vomit."

"Ew. No." I looked at her in the mirror. "Shower."

"Right," she said. "Let's get you out of this lovely T-shirt."

"I can do it myself." I protested like a five-year-old.

She stepped back but watched me for any sign that I might faint or vomit again. I faced the shower, undressed and ignored her. Stepping in, I turned on the hot water and let it pour over my head. I hoped it would cleanse the black emotions that bubbled slickly around my mind.

When I opened the shower curtain, Em was gone and a clean towel lay neatly folded on the toilet lid. Clean clothes hung on the back of the bathroom door. A glass of ice water sat on the counter beside the sink.

I dressed, brushed my teeth and toweled my hair. When I opened the door, Regulus stood in the hallway as if waiting for me to emerge.

I looked around for Em. "Is she gone?"

"Downstairs." He leaned against the wall and stared at me.

"What?"

"I like how you look when you wake."

I felt heat rush into my cheeks at the way his eyes locked with mine. The gaze felt intimate and searching. I didn't know what to do with that. The type of looks he used to give me when we'd dated. I could drown in his eyes.

I cleared my throat. "Hey. Thanks for staying, but

I'm fine now."

I took the stairs at a dangerous speed and exhaled only when I reached the bottom. Find Em. Find safety. Find a way to way to build the wall against Regulus. My heart was racing at the panic building in my chest because I knew my weakness.

"Sheriff Alder brought us food. Regulus, Emily, would you both like to stay for sandwiches?" Dad turned to get some plates from the cabinet.

"I'd like that," Regulus answered.

"Don't feel like you have to eat." I took the water that Em handed me. "I appreciate everything. Really."

I looked at Em. "You guys are the best, but it's late. I'm sure you need to go home."

"We're fine," she said.

"I'm not even hungry." I stared at the dog food bowls in the corner of the kitchen. Regulus moved to stand in front of them and I looked away.

"I'm making you a sandwich," Em said.

"She's always worked herself up like this since she was little. She internalizes everything and makes herself sick," Dad said.

"I'd like to talk with her privately after she eats," Regulus said to Dad.

"Go ahead into the dining room," Dad said. Em handed me a plate.

Regulus sat across from me at the oak table in the next room. He waited while I ate the ham and cheese sandwich. After three bites, I stopped and pushed the plate away.

"I'm fine. You guys should go."

"I'm afraid for you. I can see the sorrow in your

face. I would take it away. If I knew how..." Regulus leaned forward and ducked his head, eye level with me.

"I can't understand why Bleeker would do this. Why kill my dog? Why Nancy? To make a point to me? I hate him. I hate him with every cell in my body. Beyond hate. If the world were on fire and I—"

"Hatred will only make things more difficult." Regulus shrugged. "You must stay calm if we're to catch him."

I nodded. "Why thank you, Mister Spock." I narrowed my eyes. "So, are you and Pete in some partnership now?"

He looked at me, the words confusing him. "Mr. Spock? Partnership?"

"You didn't know each other before the wreck. He asked you to come over, right?" I pushed back in the chair.

"We talked. I would not say that we are partners." He hesitated and looked away. "Pete knows we can help each other."

"I'll talk to Pete. He'll help me get Bleeker."

"I'm here to help you."

"Well, thanks. But I don't need help. I need some sleep. OK? You're not responsible for me. I really don't want you here." I stood, rubbing my forearms.

"I came here because I knew you would be upset over Nancy even though you'd pretend not to be. And I know how much you cared about Biscuit. I came because I care about you. I care deeply."

"You care about me because...well...um...I'm your gatekeeper. It's that simple. I don't think we should be around each other more than necessary. The truth is I don't feel that way about you." I avoided his eyes.

"I know you say that, but it's not true. It is not only that you're our gatekeeper. When I saw that vehicle go over the side of mountain, I knew I'd lost something very important to me. You're more than a friend to me."

"There's nothing more," I said. "I...I don't think...I don't think we can be friends."

I struggled to get my voice under control, the squeaky high pitch that sounded unnatural in my own ears. A rushing of hurt, fear and loss swelled in my head like a tidal wave that threatened to devour me.

He stood and shook his head, taking two steps back and looking at me like I'd slapped him. He strode to the door and rested his hand on the knob for a moment. "Some people lie to others. Mia, you lie to yourself."

Chapter Thirteen

Regulus

Regulus got into Em's car, slammed the door, and texted her with the phone he'd borrowed. *"I am outside."*

"I know. B right out," she answered.

He texted. *"Hurry."* He stared at the screen, grimaced, and added a word. *"Please."*

Mia had to be the most stubborn individual he'd ever met. Did she know he could tell she lied? He wasn't a synesthete, but he'd been trained to read people.

Her bottomless brown eyes gave her away. Pupils so huge they swallowed him whole. And her voice added to the deception. She'd barely been able to speak the lies.

She thought she could depend on her brother

more than him.

Regulus thought about his Situational Analysis Training and the oddity that was Mia's brother. Peter Antares Taylor, or Pete as they called him, would have been a good IIA agent. An excellent agent if one could get past the fact that he made decisions based upon an emotional compass.

Operation Zodiac wanted Dr. Bleeker handled. An organization like OZ had no power in the politics of dimensional management. Pete obviously didn't comprehend this detail.

Regulus massaged the back of his neck with one hand. The IIA wanted Dr. Bleeker 'handled' so it would be done. It didn't matter what OZ wanted.

He'd heard lots of rumors about Pete. Rumors that the IIA had been desperate to have him. Rumors that he might be better than Mia at portal detection. The truth—not rumors—that he'd turned them down when they'd been *very* persuasive.

Unlike the lengthy conversation that Regulus got from Emily, Pete summarized what had happened in brevity. Pete had told him in a thirty second phone call what needed to be done.

Was Pete upstairs? Regulus looked at the windows at the top of the house. He thought that a bedroom had probably been Pete's once.

He glanced at Mia's window and wondered if she lay on her bed again. She'd looked so fragile and sad. Breakable. The thought of her pain unsettled him.

"Hey." Emily hopped into the driver's seat.

"She's OK?"

"No." She opened her bag and grabbed keys. "Can people our age have nervous breakdowns?"

He didn't look at her because he really didn't know the answer to that.

She barked a cynical laugh. "That was a stupid question. Of course they can."

"Emily." He looked at her frown. "Em. Mia is going to be fine." She would be. He'd make sure that of that.

"Don't act like I'm overreacting. I'm telling you that we are all she has for support right now. Her dad doesn't know the pressure she's been under since he doesn't know about the IIA and Pete and—"

"I didn't say anything. Anything about overreacting." She was making him sweat. He looked out the window again. It was too difficult to listen to her talking as if she was afraid to stop and take a breath.

"Oh, you didn't have to say anything. I can tell."

She started the car and he sighed. "Em, I know you are upset. You don't have to be upset at me."

"Uh!" she said through gritted teeth. "I'm sorry." The car lurched forward in the dark when the tires spun on the ice.

"Careful." He regretted the word when he looked at her profile. Was she smashing her lips together? "Em?"

"Yeah. I'm careful." She turned the car onto the road. "What are you going to do about this? Austin and I need to help. We want to know the plan. You think you can cut us out of what's going on, but you are so wrong."

Good. She'd assumed that he'd do something. He liked that.

"You have my word that I will capture Dr. Bleeker.

He won't be a threat to Mia again."

"I know you care about her. I do. But you need a plan. Are you waiting for him to make his next move?" Her voice grated like a marker squealing across a clean board.

He didn't share his plans with her but looked out the window instead.

"No answer, huh?" She drove the rest of the way back to his dorm in silence. She was angrier than he'd ever seen her. He watched her tap her fingers on the steering wheel during the ten mile drive. Emily had spoken her mind and he couldn't fault her for that.

She turned into the dorm parking lot in a sharp, jerky motion. Her stiff posture told him that she hadn't liked his comment on her driving, so he didn't make another.

"Thank you for taking me to Mia's," he said.

Emily nodded solemnly. "I shouldn't have snapped at you. I know you're doing the best you can."

"I am." He got out, closed the door, stepped back, and watched her taillights disappear into the distance. He rubbed the back of his neck again. He couldn't afford to have Emily shut him out. She might be his only ally when it came to reaching Mia.

"Regulus."

The low voice and the hand on his shoulder jolted him. He pivoted away and his hands formed into fists. This guy should have known better than to sneak up on him.

"Pete. Why are you here?" He narrowed his eyes and attempted to slow the rush of adrenaline.

Pete shook his head and held up both hands.

"Needed to talk and it can't wait."

"Talk."

"I called home and discovered you'd left with Em. You ready to catch Bleeker?"

"You know where he is?"

Pete gave a quick sideways nod to his truck. "Come on, before he gets away. I have orders to back off and let you take him in. I'm not happy about it, but I'd rather you get him than wait while the guys in charge decide who's the bigger dog. Jurisdiction," he added with a disgusted tone. He jogged to his truck parked a couple of spaces from them.

Melting ice shone on the parking lot from where someone had salted the pavement. Regulus walked around patches of sludge then hesitated. He trusted Pete for some reason that defied his training. Training told him to count on his teammates. Arizona sat in the room and could be summoned in minutes.

"You coming?" Pete challenged him.

"Yes." He hopped inside the warm truck. The engine was still running.

"I've tracked down his aliases and the credit cards tied to them. He's been charging on three different cards this week. He charged on one of them a half hour ago."

"Here?"

"Yeah. He leaves town, he comes back, leaves again, comes back. I can't figure out what he's doing."

"If you know where he's going, why haven't you caught him?"

"That's the problem. He's not ours. If I catch him,

I can't keep him. He's not a US citizen. He doesn't exist. I need you to take him into your custody. I want that trash gone."

"I see. Does Mia know you're here?"

Pete frowned. "No."

"She's distraught."

"You don't think I know that?"

"It's unfortunate..." He paused and searched for the best way to continue. He was supposed to say he was sorry for the untimeliness of Nancy's death. He rummaged through his brain for other appropriate terms. Condolences. Sympathy. Prayers. There was no need to finish the sentence.

Pete shook his head. "Don't."

Why did Pete deny his feelings, like Mia had? She'd denied, again and again, but he knew the death upset her.

Regulus nodded. "I think it's important to understand why he disposed of her."

"We don't have time. That's your problem. You think too much." Pete banked a left and drove off-road.

Why was Pete in a hurry to act and not plan strategy? This type of behavior could get them killed.

But he wanted to believe in Pete. Wanted to do whatever he had to do to protect Mia.

Regulus steadied himself with his hand against the dash. "Do we have a predetermined destination?"

"Do I know where we're going?" He gave a dry laugh, bordering on unstable. "Am I worrying you?"

"No." He hoped he sounded convincing. The reckless attitude had to be because of Nancy's death. Nothing else made sense or matched what he knew of Pete from the personal file he'd once read.

"Do you have answers with more than three words?"

Regulus paused. Despite wondering if he'd survive the ride to their destination, he smiled. "Only when necessary."

"I know there's a portal up ahead. I think he's been hunting for it."

"You sense the portals as adeptly as Mia?"

"Maybe better. I've been practicing." Pete's mouth formed a hard line in the glow of the dash lights.

Regulus wondered what the look meant. Maybe Pete wished he was an ordinary citizen, unaware of the intricate availability of travel between worlds. Or maybe he thought Mia should practice. He didn't ask because he guessed Pete wouldn't answer.

Pete slowed the vehicle to a crawl. "Let's park here and walk in."

"We're going to wait at the portal? How do you know he'll come?"

"He's coming. My team is herding him this way."

"To the portal?" Regulus attempted to school the surprise he felt. Pete had managed to do what he hadn't and he didn't know if he should be impressed or jealous.

"This is where you take over. I don't want him going through and getting away. We're bringing him to you. You take it from here."

Regulus was silent for a moment. The plan was one a good one. One that seemed flawless on the surface. One that would ensure the capture of Dr. Eli Bleeker. One that would keep the criminal away from Mia and her family. He could place the criminal tracking tag in Bleeker with a shot from his stunner. His apprehension would be the one merit on his record that would change his life.

In his world, an arrest of this magnitude would promote him from his current position as field agent.

His stomach churned for the first time in a while at the lack of choices before him. A promotion would mean reassignment away from Mia. She needed him.

Or did he need her? The realization bore down on him with clarity. He wanted to be with her beyond the need to please the IIA. He wanted her more than he could remember wanting anything before.

The sound of a vehicle tearing through the woods broke into his thoughts. The gunfire report rose to a deafening level.

"Are you trying to kill him?" Regulus shouted to be heard, kept his head down, and looked left and right.

"No." Pete yelled. "That's not us."

They both ducked lower when bark splintered above their heads.

He didn't understand what Pete meant. All that gun power came from Bleeker? Impossible. An armored truck spun into the clearing. The clearing that Pete had identified as a portal. Gunmen shot from the windows in a 360 degree perimeter of the vehicle.

"What's he doing?" Regulus moved to his haunches, ready to find a break in the shower of bullets. He needed to capture and tag Bleeker here. Once out of his jurisdiction, he couldn't make the arrest. He didn't have authority to tag criminals who crossed back. The thought of losing Mia and his current post had paralyzed him for a second. It was long enough for Pete to place a hand on his arm.

"Wait a minute. This is suicide. Too many guns." He shook his head in quick angry movements.

"Can't wait. Have to—" A bullet splintered wood a foot from his head. He kept his body low as he ran along the brush to get closer. Sweat dripped into his eyes.

Eli Bleeker had exited the vehicle on the other side, previously hidden from Regulus's view. The gunmen were covering the area with gunfire so Bleeker could sneak from the back to the portal opening.

He had to tag Bleeker before he made it through.

Bleeker bolted toward the portal and Regulus knew it would be close. He abandoned his cover to sprint to the armored truck. A burning sensation pierced his arm and he registered that he'd probably been hit.

He needed to stop him. He'd promised to get this killer who'd tortured Mia. A killer who wanted to use Mia and probably wouldn't stop.

Regulus lunged for Bleeker and they both breached the portal.

Chapter Fourteen

Quest

An annoying, pecking sound woke me. I groaned
and pulled the heavy quilt over my head. *Ta-ping. Ta-
ping.*

Next, my vibrating cell phone joined the chorus,
scuttling on the glass top of my bedside table. The
clock read two o'clock. I squinted to read the caller's
name. "Hello."

"Mia. It's Arizona."

"Yeah?"

"Are you awake?"

"Do I sound awake?" I sat up and looked for
Biscuit. The realization that I'd never see my dog
again suffocated me.

I sat up and put my forehead on my knees. "What
did you say?"

"I'm outside your window. I've been throwing pine
cones at your window for ten minutes."

"Why are you here?"

"Mia. Wake up. This is important." Arizona spoke in a rush.

I flung my quilt to the side and got out of bed. He had to be crazy. The temperature had dropped to ten degrees—unheard of for most winters around here. Ice with a layer of fine snow covered every surface.

At first, I couldn't see him. I turned on my light, stood in the window, and glowered at him waving frantically.

I padded across the hall to Pete's room and listened. The door was unlocked and the room silent, so I peeked inside.

The bed was empty. An avalanche of panic slid into my stomach and I inhaled sharply. A second later, I saw his duffel bag on the chair and exhaled.

He hadn't left.

After I tiptoed down the stairs, I disabled our home's security system and my shoulders drew up tight at the beeping sounds in the quiet.

Arizona didn't waste time and stepped inside. I motioned for him to follow me to my room. Not turning on any lights, I sat on the bed.

"I'll pass on being cryogenically preserved. What took you so long? " He sat beside me without waiting for invitation. Then he leaned over and swept my hair from my forehead.

"Hi." I gave a don't-worry smile. "You missed the excitement of me hurling earlier. Seems like everyone else in Whispering Woods witnessed it."

"Why didn't you take some of the medicine from my bag? It would have healed your stress. You must have a lot of bruises from the wreck on top of the shock of what's happened. I brought some with me."

"No and never."

"Mia, it's not going to hurt you. I wouldn't give you anything that would."

"I know. It's *your* medicine. As in not from earth. There's something weird about that."

He took a deep breath, rolling his eyes. "So resistant." He looked at the clock on my bedside table then back at me. "You dealing with her death?"

I noticed the way he purposely avoided the word mother."Yeah. I'm OK. I didn't even know her. She left when I was really young and she didn't care enough to take me or Pete with her."

"Right." The answer came out clipped, hurried.

"Not that I wanted her to take us. Still, I don't get why Bleeker would kill her. It doesn't make sense."

"I agree. Madmen rarely makes sense. Mia—"

"And I worry about how my brother is handling it.

"Right." Arizona placed his hand on the top mine where it rested on the bed. He lifted his other hand and rubbed his forehead. "I have something important that we need to discuss."

I narrowed my eyes. "That can't be good. What's wrong?"

"Something is very wrong."

"Is it you and Em?"

"No. I don't like to ask for help. Actually, Regulus is the only one I depend on. What happened between you two today?"

I sat staring at him. "I don't know. I said some harsh things." I hesitated for a minute. "Mean things. I know he's trying really hard to be nice to me. But he doesn't have to. I don't know if he feels some obligation to keep me happy, or if he feels guilty for what happened or—"

"Mia, we're running out of time." He was all seriousness with his end-of-the-world face. "Regulus left. He went to the Garden. He's headed toward Magnum Opus." His words tumbled out in a hurry.

I shook my head. "I don't know what you're talking about. What's Magnum Opus?"

"We don't have much time. He's traveling quickly and we need to stop him. He's not authorized."

"Is that a big deal?"

He frowned at me. "I can tell you on the way. For now, I can say that the IIA doesn't tolerate Enforcers who don't follow orders."

"Why is he doing this?"

"He's gone after Bleeker outside our jurisdiction." He shook his head. "He's going to get himself arrested to prove something to you or Pete or…I don't know. He's crazy."

"Arrested? Did you say Pete? What does Pete have to do with this?"

"I called Em and then your brother because I was trying to locate Regulus. Your brother took him with his team to apprehend Bleeker. There was some kind of struggle and Regulus and Bleeker went through the portal."

I stood, holding my breath. "We'll stop him. What can I do?"

Arizona took both my hands. "I need your help, for you to be fully committed to getting him back."

I hesitated, my mind whirling. Arizona's fear tasted of tart raspberries. Had I ever seen him afraid?

I remembered another time. Regulus had been near death from a biological weapon meant to kill me.

"We can follow him. Stop him." I grabbed his hand and rubbed his wrist to feel the location chip inserted underneath the skin. "You know exactly where he is."

"Not when he's off this plane."

"This plane?"

"I have to be in the same dimension. Or I can't. He's gone home."

Arizona saw a backpack in the corner of the room. He handed it to me and grabbed my free hand. "We'll be right back. I'll have you back in an hour."

He tugged me toward the door.

I pulled back. "Let me talk to my dad and tell him that...that..." I closed my eyes and inhaled, trying to get enough air into my lungs. "He needs to know when I'll be back. He's stressed enough as it is. I can't make him worry."

"What if I promised you that we'd be back before he notices you're gone?" He grabbed my new pink cell phone which he quickly slung into the backpack.

"You're sure?" When he didn't answer, I took his chin and forced him to make eye contact with me.

"Time is different than you think. It will not be a problem. You have my word." He gave me that confident smile I expected. The confident one that he hadn't shown since entering my bedroom. It always worked for him.

Arizona pushed. "I've spent too much time explaining this. Decide. Come or I'm leaving without you." The smile was gone and he slung my backpack onto his shoulder. He rushed to the stairs without looking back.

"I'm coming."

I watched him go into my kitchen. Cabinets sounded like they were opening and closing while I grabbed my coat from the rack in the entry. Adding gloves and a hat, I hesitated again and looked toward the kitchen.

Arizona sped around the corner, took a quick look at me, nodded approvingly, and opened the door.

"Come on, my little gatekeeper."

* * *

"It's up ahead," I said, gritting my teeth against a gust of sharp wind that made my skin burn. I pushed the wool scarf closer to my neck and over half my face before I exhaled warm air to thaw my nose. The frozen ground sparkled with a layer of snow and ice.

If not for the buzz I felt in approaching the portal, I would have thought every living thing on earth was asleep. The stillness was deceptive until I looked ahead to the area near our creek and felt the vibrations undulating like heat over a highway.

Arizona didn't appear to mind the cold like I did. He'd turned up the collar on his ski jacket but didn't wear gloves.

"You nervous about going through?"

His words were low and I knew he didn't care if I was nervous or not. He walked at a pace that had me practically running.

"Well, I'm not. I'm trying to not think about it. Talking about it isn't helping." I stepped in a hole and recovered with an ungraceful, half-falling lunge.

He never slowed.

"The other time you went through, we were on motorcycles. This time, we aren't. There are reasons for that and you'll see soon enough. I don't have time to explain everything to you, but you do need to keep up. I can't babysit you."

"I figured that part out already." I rolled my eyes. He couldn't see me, but I didn't like this side of Arizona. The all-business-boss-Mia-around sort. He was like Regulus plus six cups of coffee. This jittery Arizona needed to chill.

He stopped short of the periphery of the portal. The banded circle of vibrating air emitted a high pitched chorus of sound. He checked his cell phone.

"What are you doing? Checking your Portal Finder app?" I said, expecting an overbearing answer from this new version of Arizona.

The corner of his mouth kicked up in a condescending tilt and he grabbed my hand. "No, I wanted to check the GPS app for the portal location."

He couldn't see or feel the portal. Sometimes, I forgot that everyone couldn't, except for synesthetes. The sounds and tingles along my spine excited me like running after fireflies as a kid. Chasing their glowing bodies had been irresistible.

The fireflies of my youth were long gone and I'd rarely found that thrill in the woods during my teen years. Finding portals had been a surprising escape.

"You could've asked." I shook my head and I stared at the space ahead.

"Yeah, well, I'm not crazy about women drivers."

"Very funny."

"Actually, it is." He nudged me with an elbow.

"Ready? Because here we go. Don't let go of my hand."

He gripped my hand tighter and yanked forward. It surprised me like a hard sneeze, uncontrollable and sudden.

Inside the portal, my stomach bottomed out. It slammed into my gut again. My lips ached; I'd bitten the bottom one on impact. I ran my fingers along my lips to see if blood wet my mouth. My head throbbed like it had in yesterday's car wreck.

I forced my eyes open, expecting bright sunlight, burning pain, something, anything, that would match the shock of the moment of entry into this other world.

Instead I looked down to see wet pavement littered with trash. "Same alley?"

"What?" He was genuinely confused at my question.

"Is this the same alley as before? When you and Regulus brought me?"

"Shh..." He pulled me into the shadow of a dumpster.

My entire being ached from yesterday and today hadn't helped matters. But only inside my head did I protest the manhandling. We slipped from the shadow of the dumpster to hide behind a fire escape platform running down the right side of the building.

A fresh pile of feces sat on the lowest platform beside my head. I fought the gagging that automatically choked me at the stench. Only something newly deposited would steam in the cold, damp, night air.

Arizona pulled his jacket collar up higher to touch

his chin. The sound of pounding feet made me jerk my head up. He turned toward me. His wide green eyes and the tiniest movement of his head from left to right warned against speaking.

Men—ten or so—ran with pounding uniformity past the alley, holding translucent, molded shields to their chests. Their headgear looked like hockey masks and they wore tall, black boots.

Once they were gone, Arizona held one finger to his lips and grabbed my hand. He leaned forward and kissed me on the mouth. It was a quick kiss, over before I realized what he intended to do.

"We did it. We're in." He gave me that familiar grin I'd seen so often with him. Carefree and happy.

His statement drew my immediate attention. "I didn't know that getting here was debatable," I said. Then I remembered the kiss. "And why did you do that?" I rubbed my mouth across my sleeve.

He shrugged. "I was caught up in the moment. You know—the thrill. Sorry about that."

He wore smug expression and there wasn't an ounce of sorry in his twinkling eyes.

"You are an adrenaline junkie." I stated and glanced around. "This doesn't look like the place we went before," I said.

"It's not. I told you where we were going." He rounded the corner and glanced back to make sure I was right behind him.

"Oh," I answered as if I knew. He'd said some names that meant nothing to me.

"I'm counting on you to get us out of here. We have two hours before this portal will close."

"Huh?" The hairs on the back of my neck bristled.

Arizona leaned forward to give me a look that demanded I pay attention then spoke in a clipped voice. "Fact. Portals disappear and new ones open up in Whispering Woods and in every dimension. Fact. You are able to locate the new ones before the IIA can. Fact. This is the reason you're called the Gatekeeper."

I mimicked his know-it-all tone. "Fact. This didn't mean much to me until today and you never told me about the portals here."

We skimmed the walls like secret agents, walking as quickly as possible without actually breaking into a run. Every building appeared to be a skyscraper, rising to an impossibly dark sky. A searchlight from a rooftop illuminated a swath of building fronts near us.

My breath came in shallow pants. "How much farther? Does your thing..." I pointed at my wrist to indicate the chip. "Does it work now?"

He nodded. "Do I need to slow down?" He stopped to look me full in the face. "Are you sick?" He put his hands on both my shoulders.

"I don't know. I'm tired from finding out about Biscuit. And the wreck." My face felt clammy. Saying Biscuit's name made my chest ache. "And the barfing."

"Barfing?" The corner of his mouth lifted as if he enjoyed the new vocabulary, something he'd obviously missed in his language training.

I squinted and glared at his question.

"Sorry. I find that word funny. You should take the meds I tried to give you earlier. It will make you feel better. Immediately."

"I don't want—"

"Mia. We don't have time to argue. I'm not sure if it's stress or a stomach bug, but you need to get better now."

"Fine." I held out my hand. He reached into the backpack that hung over his shoulder, the one he'd taken from my room. Removing a box, he carefully opened the lid and took out a thin, blue square, one-half inch in diameter.

I knew the drill.

"Below the tongue. Let it dissolve."

I nodded and obliged. No burn or taste of chemicals. No zinging through my blood like I'd expected. No high.

"Is Regulus near?" I hoped that Arizona's implanted sensor chip was singing. This world with its dark streets filled me with dread.

"He's a couple of miles ahead." Arizona took a right and we scurried across an intersection. Overhead, a large metal arch announced the entrance to a district in letters too dark to read. Throngs of people walked in both directions. There were no vehicles and I realized I hadn't seen one since we'd arrived.

"I'm still woozy, but I think I feel better. Walk faster." I grabbed the back of his nylon jacket to make sure I didn't lose him.

The sardine-can feeling progressively worsened as we entered the second block of the district. Heavy darkness pressed on me from the people, from the buildings, from the air.

I could feel the tension vibrating around as Arizona led me forward. A man with a dirty face grabbed my arm and I squealed, jerked back and tried to escape his grasp. Arizona turned and glared at the man. The stranger slumped to the ground and I saw the stunner in Arizona's hand.

"Don't let go." He turned back around, continuing to push his way through the bodies.

A thumping sound penetrated the air and I realized it was the same sound we'd heard in the alley. People yelled and chanted. Arizona moved to the left between buildings. He ran and I could barely keep my grip on his coat. After noticing my struggle, he pivoted and grabbed my hand in a pinching grip.

Again, we hid, but this time behind a large metal box stamped with strange letters and an insignia.

"What is going on?" I asked through clenched teeth.

"Nothing. Normal." He hesitated for a beat too long and I sensed that there was something not quite right with his tone or eyes.

"Why are we hiding?" I inched past the metal box and he yanked me back, hard.

"You aren't authorized to be here. They can't identify you without a chip."

I schooled my expressions so he couldn't see how scared I'd suddenly become. "The IIA?" The two words came out a little low, but I controlled the shaking I felt inside.

"Actually, the Makers don't know. I mean, the IIA...they don't know either. If they find us, they'll insert your chip. But we'll be out of here in no time." His demeanor was serious. Calm. A little too calm.

I'd always known Arizona to never be afraid, never unsure, never worried. Everything I'd known about him was wrong. A mossy green frisson of color surrounded him and told me that we were in trouble.

His denying it chilled me to the core.

"Do they know you're here?"

"Yes."

I grabbed both his upper arms. "So, you're authorized and this is routine? Your being here?"

"The IIA may wonder why I'm in the Garden, but it's no big deal."

I knew he was lying.

I chose to ignore it for the moment. "Is Regulus very far ahead now?"

"He's keeping a steady pace, but he's fast. We're fine. He's near the border of Magnum Opus."

"What's that?" I asked. He pulled me from behind the metal box. I glanced at the emblem painted on it; it reminded me of a radioactive waste emblem.

"It's a sanctioned facility, level ten. A place where the Makers cure the ills of the worlds."

"Huh." I opened my mouth to ask another question, but promptly shut it. I could sense that he didn't want me asking questions and I was too out of breath to ask more, if I wanted to keep up.

"Regulus can't go in because he doesn't have an invitation." Arizona exited the narrow alley from the opposite direction where we'd entered. This new street was darker than the last. Arizona dropped my hand. I wished he hadn't, but I didn't intend to act like I needed it.

"Don't move from this spot," Arizona said. "I'll be back in a minute."

My stomach cramped and a clammy sweat stole over my face. "Hurry."

Chapter Fifteen

Caregiver

The ringing in my ears matched the pounding of Arizona's feet. I knew I was sicker than I'd been at my house. I tried to remember if I'd ever been this sick before.

"Mia. Mia?"

I heard Arizona was calling my name and I saw him waving his hand to me from the end of the alley. Arizona's face blurred and I bent over with my elbows on my knees.

A hand rested on my back.

"Pete?" Sweat beaded on my upper lip.

"Mia, it's me. You're confused. I don't know why the meds didn't work. Sit down."

Obeying him was easy because I wanted to fall down. I leaned against the concrete wall and slid to the ground. "I'm down."

"We can't stay here. I have to move you. Take a

minute and breathe."

"I can get up." I moaned when I attempted to slide up the wall. It didn't work as well as sliding down.

"You're very hot." Arizona shifted my arm over his shoulder for support. He grabbed me around the waist and lifted me.

"I'm hot?" I laughed deliriously. "Why thank you. Really. You're pretty hot yourself."

"Ssh. I've got to get us out of here. Lean on me and we're going back into the streets." He placed the scarf I'd worn over my head.

"Why are you covering my hotness?" I knew I was babbling. In the recesses of my mind, I knew something was very wrong, but I was afraid to stop talking.

"I'll get help. Don't worry."

Arizona's whispering at my ear made me wonder if he felt uncomfortable taking care of me and it made me wonder if I should feel uncomfortable that he was definitely in my personal space. I realized it didn't matter. My thoughts were running wild in my fuzzy brain. Disorganized. I wondered if I might be dying.

My knees buckled and he picked me up. I tucked my face against his chest. He knocked on a door; his raps were hard and impatient. I heard the door open.

"My friend is sick," Arizona said. "I've run out of meds. I need your help."

"Come," the person said.

Arizona moved again and placed me on a hard surface. "I've given her meds and they aren't working. Maybe more will help? I don't know. I don't understand it."

My arm muscles didn't cooperate with my brain

firing orders. I lifted one fingertip.

"Can you bring a scientist?" Arizona asked.

"I will bring him."

"Thank you," I said. The woman before me was older with gray hair and soft blue eyes.

"Is she your pair?" the woman asked. She left the room then returned with cold, wet cloths.

"No." Arizona leaned down, squeezed my forearm, then patted my head. "I'm here. You'll live."

"Living is a good thing," I whispered and gave one short laugh. He probably wasn't making an understatement.

A while later, the woman returned with an elderly man.

"How long has she been ill?" He placed his hand on my cheek.

"Today," Arizona said. "Not...um...longer. She was sick earlier. She said she vomited yesterday."

The man busied himself with things from a bag he'd brought. I watched him through half-opened eyes. He reminded me of an older version of my dad, patient and calm.

"She is not a citizen," the man said.

Arizona froze. He seemed unsure.

I answered for him. "No."

The man nodded. "I'm Josah." He gave a tight smile, his mouth closed and sad. "I was like you once."

Arizona touched my hand.

"And you are a citizen." Josah stared at him. "What are you doing with her?"

"I'm an Enforcer."

Josah raised one eyebrow. "That would be a

problem."

"She's my friend. I am responsible for her. You are helping her, not me."

Josah leaned forward. "Let us see what I can do. I need to test something." He removed an object from his case. "Move her into a sitting position."

Arizona placed his arm behind my back and pushed. "Does she need to stay upright? Should she sit in a chair?"

"No. It will be over in a minute." He held a clear ball between his fingers. "I am going to ask you to hold this ball inside your mouth. I will take it from you in two minutes."

I nodded that I understood and opened my mouth. The smooth ball felt like an oversize marble in my mouth. A bead of sweat trickled from my forehead and into my eyes, forcing me to blink away the stinging sensation.

Josah held a cup to my mouth. "Place it in the cup."

The desire to sleep chugged toward me like a train barreling at a steady speed. I spit the ball into the cup and slumped back.

"Catch her," Josah said.

* * *

I woke to Arizona's voice. "It's time to wake."

Liquid trickled into my mouth and choked me. I coughed and gagged. A burning sensation filled my mouth and I sputtered. "Hey. Stop." If he didn't stop putting the cup to my lips, he was going to drown me.

"You'll get dehydrated."

I held out shaky hands to take the cup from him. He held my shoulders.

The room was dark, but light seeped in around the edges of the window. "Is it night?"

"No. Morning. We've been here a day."

I jerked upright and looked around. "Here?" A blanket lay carelessly thrown across a chair beside the bed. "I'm not sure what's happened. Is this the same place you brought me when I was sick?"

"Uh-huh. Same."

"What about Regulus?"

"He's still close. I don't know what he's doing, but he's not moving farther away."

"You decided to wake." The woman came in with a pitcher and glass. She nodded at Arizona. "Take a break. I'll watch her."

"I don't need a break." Arizona gave her an irritated look.

"Go. You never listen."

Their exchange confused me. *Never* listen?

Arizona shrugged. "I'll stretch my legs. Mia, I'm not going far." He left the room and the woman sat on the chair.

"Thank you. For everything. I'm Mia."

"I'm Caregiver."

"Caregiver," I repeated. "That's an odd name."

"Mia is an odd name."

I smiled. "I guess it is." I stared at her staring back at me.

"Do you know Arizona? I mean, from before yesterday?" It was a hunch. Caregiver had such a pleasant face. Her blue eyes were warm and sparkled with intelligence and understanding.

"Of course I do. I know Regulus, too. I cared for both of them while they trained at The Vault."

"Ah." I smiled and my silly heart raced at hearing his name.

"And are you a pair for Regulus?"

I kept smiling. "I don't know what you mean. A pair?"

"The Makers haven't placed you, have they?"

My insides began to flutter nervously. "No." I wished Arizona would return.

"Arizona will take you to them."

I steadied my breathing. "Why would he do that?"

She held out her hand. When I didn't move, she said, "Let me hold your hand."

A cold spike of dread started in my chest and traveled to my hand, rendering it immobile. She waited and I stretched my fingers toward hers.

"What are you doing?" Arizona didn't sound like his usual happy self.

"I'm...uh..." I darted my eyes from him to Caregiver. She still had her hand out.

"Mia. Get ready to go. We're leaving," Arizona ordered.

Caregiver smiled at me for the first time. It was an apologetic smile. It suddenly hit me that she gave nothing to be read. No vibes or colors that I could determine.

"I hope you take care of her, Arizona. She is different."

"Yes. She is." Arizona picked up my scarf and coat lying across the end of the bed.

"I wanted to ask her for more information,"

Caregiver said.

"Your translator works fine so you can ask her out loud," Arizona said. "But really, there's nothing more that you should know."

Something was going on, but I couldn't figure it out. I'd remember to ask Arizona later. I swung my feet to the floor and looked around for my bag. "Please tell Mr. Josah thank you."

"I will." Caregiver walked us to the door. "Goodbye, Arizona."

He didn't even turn around. I elbowed him, but he ignored me.

"Bye, Caregiver." We stepped outside. "What's up with you?"

"Nothing." He looked at me like I'd said something stupid.

"You were so rude to her."

"No, I wasn't." He grinned at me. "You don't know, do you?"

"Know what?" I hurried to keep up with his long strides.

"I guess I thought you'd know. Or be able to tell. I have no idea what Regulus has told you and what he hasn't."

"Told me what?"

He looked around as if someone might overhear our conversation. "She's an artificial."

"Artificial? Artificial what?"

"She's not human."

I stopped, my feet cemented in place. "Not human? She seemed human to me."

"She has some superior human tissues. I don't know the reason for that. But her brain is a computer." He grabbed my hand to pull me forward.

I shook my hand from his and continued walking. I'd felt better before this information. Now, I was queasy all over again. It must have shown because Arizona halted.

"I thought you were cured?"

"I feel fine. Did Josah do something to me?"

"He gave you a shot. He also diagnosed that you've been poisoned."

If I hadn't wanted to sit before, I did now. Seeing that Arizona walked like he was late to catch a plane, I kept pace with him.

"I can't handle this. Artificial people. Somebody poisoning me. It's too much."

He stopped and turned to me. "You had something in your system that Josah diagnosed. A bacteria that causes a chemical imbalance in your body."

"Like the flu?"

"No. Strains of the flu abound in your world. They've been identified and documented. This bacterium was different."

"How so?"

"It originated here."

I grabbed his elbow. "But that's not possible."

He held up the bag. "Josah asked me if I knew what you'd been eating. I laughed at first because there's no way I'd know. He said something about it being mixed with citric acid in your stomach."

I frowned at him. "So?"

"At your house, I grabbed food to throw in this bag. One thing I grabbed was a tin of that stuff you offered me at your house on Christmas Eve. Fruitcake? The food I didn't want to try because it looked too odd."

"What about it?"

"The poison was in the fruitcake. Where did you get that?"

"It was a Christmas gift on our front porch. I don't know." I stumbled at the disgusted look he gave me. "Don't look at me like that."

"Do you eat everything you find? Someone left it for you and it seemed safe to eat?"

"People give us baked goods for Christmas every holiday. It's..."

He waited for me to finish.

"...I was going to say normal. But really it's stupid."

"Are you the only one who ate it?" he asked.

"Yeah. My dad hates that stuff. And you saw how no one touched it the other night. I've always loved it."

"I'm trying to figure out who poisoned it. Nancy? Bleeker? I don't know."

"I could have died. Bleeker didn't want to kill me. I think he didn't..."

"It would break down your resistance until someone here could give you treatment. Treatment like Josah gave you. Otherwise it would have eventually killed you. But it would take a little while. Enough time for someone to offer treatment in exchange for something that he wanted."

We'd reached a building with an elevator on the outside. The car was moving up at racecar speed. Arizona stopped and turned to me. "We're going in."

"Why?"

"Woman, I need resources. Money. Food." He

sighed.

I followed him inside. "About Caregiver. You already knew her."

"She was my caregiver."

"Like a nanny?"

"Maybe."

"And Regulus's?"

"Uh-huh." He turned a corner and walked into a huge circular area. A rotating walk moved around the perimeter and people stepped on and off.

Arizona stepped on, and I followed.

"What did she do for you?"

"She made sure I had rations, knew how to navigate the world, and had someone to talk to."

"Like a mother?"

He laughed. "Better than a mother."

"How's that?"

"Never told me no."

"That's sad. I mean if you're OK with not having someone care if you get hurt or feel down..."

He stared at me with a smirk. "You didn't have a mother to do those things."

"But I had my dad."

"Here. Exit." The smooth white walls gleamed like polished floors, an illuminated circle appearing every twelve inches. Arizona pressed his finger to a circle that looked like the others.

A drawer slid out. Arizona scanned his wrist over the center of opened drawer and I waited to see what would happen next.

An alarm sounded, high and piercing.

He shoved the drawer shut with one hand, grabbed my hand with the other, skipped the moving walkway, and ran. "They've frozen my resources. Fast. Run fast!"

The entrance to the building was clogged with people who appeared to be looking for someone. Someone pointed at us and Arizona pulled my arm harshly. My lungs nearly burst when we hit the street, our feet pounding against the pavement.

I shot a glance over my shoulder and saw three men chasing us. They'd catch us very soon. If I let go of Arizona's hand, he could make it. On impulse, I relaxed my grip but Arizona held on tighter.

"I. Said. Fast." He turned a corner, entered a building, slid around corners. I had no choice but to keep up.

We exited through a door and came up against a brick wall. Arizona released my hand and jumped. His fingers caught the top edge and he pulled himself up.

"Jump."

"I can't make it."

He straddled the top and reached down. "Grab my hand. Do it."

I jumped and caught his hand. He slung me to the top. My arms stretched to their limit and my joints screamed a protest. I tumbled over and dropped to the other side.

Once I landed, I stumbled back and my head hit the ground.

* * *

I woke to darkness. A single light swung lazily, like a clock pendulum. I saw more lights in a string above my head. Tilting my head, I saw millions of lights. Christmas, I thought.

"I had this nightmare," I croaked. I closed my eyes again. The hand that took mine was vaguely familiar, but not Dad's.

"Hmm..." The response sounded far away.

I registered noise and wondered if the television volume could be lowered. Something cool pressed upon my forehead. Fingers touched my lips and I protested, trying to sit.

"Hello." The masculine voice tickled my ears. Its tone reverberated pleasantly. Not nasally, but low and comforting. Powerful.

"Hello," I mimicked with a faint smile and no attempt to open my eyes. I tried to remember what had happened and failed. "Go away."

"Help her sit. Is she awake?" The second masculine voice was pleasant, but not like the first.

"She's awake. I think she is ignoring us." The last part was said with a smile. I could tell.

I pried my eyes open again and the lights burned them as I focused. A dark head moved to shield the light. I stared into dark blue eyes that made my stomach tingle.

Bottomless. Mysterious. Dangerous.

I broke the gaze and saw another person leaning over me. "Where am I?" I scooted over to avoid touching the one seated nearest my side.

Arizona answered me with a rueful grin. "We barely made it out alive. I don't know why they've triggered my box. It's a good thing Regulus doubled back."

"Where?" I rubbed my forehead.

"Underground. About a mile from where you dropped and hit your head. I thought you'd land on your feet."

I bolted upright. "Where am I again?" I sat on a pile of cardboard boxes stacked four feet high and the width of a twin bed.

I was fine, but dazed. Regulus put hands on both my shoulders. I wiggled back to remove myself from his grasp, which wasn't difficult. His hands fell to his sides.

"Mia, it's OK. You're confused." He stared with those eyes that made me want to look away before he emptied my mind of every secret thought I'd ever had. He wouldn't break the stare and as much as I tried, I couldn't either. We were trapped trying to read each other, scared to look away and lose the connection.

"Regulus." Arizona placed a hand on the shoulder of the one seated by my side. "That knock to the head may be serious."

I traced my fingertips over the back of my head. "My head has a bump," I mumbled and recognized a fuzzy sensation.

Regulus turned to Arizona. "I cannot believe you brought her here. You've done this to her. I'm holding you responsible." He stood then paced in a circle that made me dizzy.

"Hello?" My irritation grew with each second. "Is anyone going to answer me? I don't know where we are, why you thought you could capture Bleeker by yourself, or...or...why my head hurts like I've been hit by Thor's hammer."

I watched Arizona give me an enormous grin.

"Well, darlin', we are here to save the day. To make sure Regulus makes it back home and doesn't try anymore of these macho stunts again. To—"

A second later, Regulus slammed Arizona against the nearest wall. "That's for disobeying the rules."

"Stop it!" I yelled when they began scuffling in earnest. Arizona put his fist into Regulus's side when he couldn't get loose.

"And this is for bringing her to the Garden." Regulus released Arizona's jacket and landed a punch against his jaw. Arizona lunged and tackled him to the ground.

"Hey," I yelled again, but no one listened. I could have been yelling into a black hole. I jumped up to stop them without regard for my actions or how stupid they might be.

They rolled twice and Regulus came out on top. I grabbed his coat and pulled until he paid attention to me.

Finally he stopped. He stood, brushed off his clothes then offered his hand to Arizona. Regulus pulled him halfway up, released his hand then let Arizona fall back to the concrete floor.

"And in Mia's words, that was because you get on my last nerve."

Chapter Sixteen

Down the Hole

"Are you finished?" I asked.

The sound of Arizona breathing like he'd run a 5k filled the alcove of what could have been a concrete parking garage or storage basement or underground bunker. I could only guess from its deserted appearance. Spooky, but clean. My relief disappeared a moment later when something scurried across the room, forcing me to pull my feet up from the floor and tuck them under my knees.

The lights indicated that the building had to be in use, and I was glad for that. I didn't relish the thought of being locked in the dark.

"I might as well tell you this while you're still mad." Arizona wiped his arm dramatically across his nose.

Regulus nodded but didn't answer.

"I lost my weapon above ground." Arizona waited a beat. "And Mia's bag. So..." he waited for Regulus to say something.

The buzzing lights hummed in a steady tone. Regulus still didn't answer or look at either one of us.

"You haven't answered my questions," I muttered.

"You can hit me again," Arizona whispered. "I know. I know. I thought this would be easy. I brought her in case we needed to get out fast and she could get us to a portal."

"Mia, you don't have to worry. I'll take care of you," Regulus said. "We'll get you home."

My face must have answered him.

"You're not scared, right?" he continued in the calm way like trying to talk someone off a ledge.

"No. Maybe a little. Tell me where we are and how I can call my dad. I need my phone." I hated the whine in my voice.

"Of course we'll tell you that," Regulus said.

Arizona stood peering around the corner and didn't turn his head at the words he tossed over his shoulder. "We're not alone."

Regulus grabbed me by the waist and lifted me then deposited me on my feet. "We might be in trouble with some people who will hurt us. It's important that you follow my lead. Understand?"

I nodded. His eyes held mine with that earnest kind of look I couldn't help but trust. A look that spelled safety and strength. A look that I'd follow anywhere.

Regulus signaled the direction with a slight nod. He had to be crazy. Maybe I could trust him but not his judgment.

"On the count of three," Regulus said. "One—"

"Three," called Arizona.

I had one second to balance myself then pushed off with the ball of my back foot. Regulus grabbed my hand, jerked me roughly forward, then ran off with me. Rounding the corner, I gasped at the legion approaching us. It was a second of vision, no more, but enough to make me run hard. Thousands of tiny specks of light crawled toward us. The sight mesmerized me momentarily and then I was racing next to Regulus.

"Go," I screamed. Without a doubt, Regulus was holding back, running slowly to keep me within his peripheral vision.

"You go," he yelled and grabbed my hand. Arizona scaled a wall of metal scrap ahead of us. He made it look effortless.

I jumped, hit the wall and fell back when my feet didn't find their target.

Regulus glanced back and stalled. Twisting his entire torso, he grabbed for my hand again.

My body banged against the barrier before he lifted me to him.

"Through here." Arizona darted into a hole in the crumbling wall.

I crawled like a crab into the hold after him. Regulus followed then pulled something heavy to the entrance. Breathing roughly, I leaned my forehead against the brick.

"No time to rest," he urged. "You don't want the Rovers on us."

"I—"

"Run," Arizona yelled with a flushed, horrified look marring his face.

Crawling quickly was the best we could do. The tunnel we'd entered was filled with debris of the best unknown variety. Brown, black, and gray tones made for a dirt colored escape hole that made me feel like a rat scurrying down a maze.

My stomach roiled at smells that forced to me to hold my breath until no longer possible.

"How much farther?" I whispered to anyone who would listen.

Arizona stopped in front of me. His hand shot out and covered my mouth. "Rovers can't hear us, but we don't want any others looking either."

Regulus had stopped close to me. His warm breaths tickled my neck and sent nervous chills up my spine. "We need to find a way out of here."

"Who are you running from?" I said in a hoarse whisper.

"No, we. We are running," Regulus corrected.

The grating sound of metal against metal pierced my ears. I put both hands over them and squeezed my eyes.

"Come on." Arizona's voice was strangled. He motioned with a hurried rolling of the fingers.

It occurred to me that I wasn't sure why I was running or who might catch me or if that would be bad. I only sensed their urgency and fear. So, I followed.

My head grazed some low concrete and I ducked. Light shone ahead—Arizona had already exited through a small opening. I grunted and rolled out onto a drop of a few feet that felt like more.

Regulus's hand on my waist meant he'd made it through. Glancing back, I wasn't sure how his size had permitted his exit; he was much larger than I.

Arizona led the way and I followed through dark alleys until he stopped abruptly.

"What's wrong? Why are we stopping?" I looked from one of my guides to the other.

"How do you know she's still here?" Regulus said to Arizona. He'd ignored my question as if I weren't there.

"I don't." Arizona searched the ground. "I don't know a thing more than you, but it's our only chance."

"Who are we looking for?" I scanned the ground that was probably paved at one time but now consisted of broken concrete with grass and mud holding it together.

"Stand back." Regulus's tone wasn't unpleasant, but the order was definite.

"I demand an answer." I refused to move from my spot and folded my arms across my chest.

"She's back to her normal self," Arizona said.

"That's it. I'm going." I suddenly wanted to cry but made no move to actually leave. It would be ludicrous to head off in a direction when I had no idea where I'd go.

"Hey, I was kidding." Arizona put a hand on my shoulder. I shrugged and his hand fell away.

"Listen. I'm going home. Got it? Point me in the right direction." I needed to stop my voice from quivering.

They exchanged looks. Then, Regulus nodded to me. "We have to hide until we can get to a portal." His voice was gentle, persuasive.

I inhaled deeply, telling myself that I had more

guts than the whimpering person I was a second ago.

"I'm OK," I said.

Regulus grabbed my arm and jerked me against his chest.

"Holy sinkhole, Batman." A huge, gaping hole appeared in the earth where I'd been standing seconds earlier.

"Down the hole." Regulus gave my arm a reassuring squeeze. When I didn't move, he added, "You won't be going home if you're captured."

A ladder descended into the darkness to a point below.

"You first." I nodded at him. My brave factor had dissolved in the last ten minutes; I didn't want to drop into the depths of the unknown.

"You second. Arizona, last," Regulus replied without looking my way. He climbed down and I had no choice but to follow. Arizona herded me to the hole. One foot on the ladder down and a gust of cool wind swirled around my legs.

At the bottom, I couldn't see a thing. "You there?"

"Here," he answered in my ear.

I stuck my hand out and found his body beside mine. He took my hand and I gladly clung to it.

The door above closed with an eerie silence.

"You guys making out? Because I'm feeling alone over here."

I had to laugh. "Um, no. I can't see you. I'm afraid to move."

"You should be afraid," a strange voice answered.

I jumped and bright lights burned my eyes.

"It's me. Arizona," the voice beside me said. "I'm friends with Cassie."

"Friends?" a husky feminine voice questioned.

"Cassie?" Arizona said with a smile I could hear.

I shielded my eyes with one hand. Uneasiness tickled my spine. No one said a word. The 1000-watt light had to be pointed directly into my eyes. I wondered if they thought they were trying to light a baseball field with that lamp. I'd be seeing spots for a while.

An object pressed against the back of my head.

"Place your hands behind your back," a male voice said. The object tapped my head.

"Hey," I said before I could stop myself.

"Do what he says." Regulus spoke in a calm, fearless way that I envied.

My belly fluttered in uneasiness and my breathing quickened.

"Cassie, you should be more careful of the company you keep," Arizona said. I heard scuffling and knew he'd been restrained. My eyes were adjusting to the bright light and I could see a group surrounded us.

"Where did you find her?" A petite girl with sharp eyes assessed me from head to toe.

"She's a nobody. We met her a day or two ago," Regulus said.

"And that would be why you are watching her so closely, eh?" the smooth female voice behind me said.

"Good or evil? Good or evil?" chanted another girl.

"Cassie." The teasing had disappeared from Arizona's voice, now taut and urgent. "Come on, is this really necessary? We're friends."

The click of a cuff around Arizona's wrists

disagreed.

"You left in the middle of the night." She led the way with her hand on Arizona's elbow. "I've had enemies treat me with more respect."

We proceeded in silence down a dark passage with a low ceiling. A woman behind Cassie held a bright sphere that lit our footpath.

We turned so many corners that I lost count and consequently realized we'd never find our way back to the entrance.

The destination appeared to be a series of cells. Glass doors allowed complete view of the insides. Solid side walls prevented the prisoners from speaking to each other.

Cassie pushed Arizona into one harder than necessary and he stumbled. A tall, slim man indicated that I should enter the same cell.

"No." Cassie's voice was razor sharp. "Not there." When a woman attempted to guide Regulus to the same room as Arizona, Cassie shook her head. "Not those two together."

"We don't have enough room," protested the man. Cassie opened the door to the neighboring cell. "Those two in here." She nodded her head to the right and I obeyed.

Inside, I faced the back wall. The only furniture was a twin bunk with a thin mattress and blanket.

"This is inconvenient." I turned to look at my cellmate. "No bathroom."

His mouth teased upward at one corner. The cot looked clean enough, so I sat on the edge. "What do we do now?"

"Good question." He tapped gently on the wall. An

answering tap made Regulus smile.

"Why are they holding us? Was she an old girlfriend of his?" I jerked my head to indicate Arizona in the neighboring room.

"Not to my knowledge." The answer shot out quickly.

"Yeah. They were a thing."

His brows rose at my statement. "And how do you know this?"

"Believe me. They had to be something for She-ra to be so mad. She had that vengeance look in her eyes. The look that said she'd like to cover him with paper cuts before sprinkling him with salt."

He didn't reply. Instead, he circled the room, studying all surfaces, picking with his fingernail at the seamless way the bed attached to the floor. Finally, he sighed with what might have been all the air in his lungs and sat propped against the wall.

"I thought you wanted us to work as I team. You left. Alone. You suck at teamwork." I sat on the hard bunk with my knees drawn up under my chin.

"You haven't been very interested in working with Arizona and me lately. I needed to get Bleeker while I could."

I didn't answer immediately, but chose my words carefully. "I never said I didn't want to help get Bleeker. I'm not interested in working for the IIA. There's a difference."

"We have the same objectives. They want us to be an efficient team. It's the reason why they have the rules they do. Does that help you understand?"

I shook my head. "Not so much. If they had wanted us to be a close team, they wouldn't have messed with your head."

Regulus opened his mouth but appeared to change his mind about speaking. He rubbed both hands down his face and left them over his mouth. "You don't understand," he said quietly.

"True." I sat back, closed my eyes and listened for sounds that seemed nonexistent.

"Tired?"

"Yes," I whispered. The tenderness in his voice made my throat tighten.

"May I ask you something?"

I peered sidelong without turning my head to see he'd inched closer. "What?"

"Tell me where we left our relationship."

"Huh? I don't know what you mean." I began chewing on my thumbnail. It throbbed so I forced both hands between my knees.

"I think you do."

"Can we talk about something else?" I put my head back on my knees. "I'm sorry I brought it up. Really sorry." I banged my head once on my knees and sat in a tight little ball.

"Um..."

I left my forehead on my knees and waited for him to finish. Finally, I looked up to meet his eyes. "What?"

"Your mother. You want to talk about her?"

"Not really." I barely kept the tremor out of my answer.

"I know for fact that you had no relationship with her."

"That's right. I didn't."

"Did you want one?"

"No. And actually, it's none of your business. The woman is dead. It wouldn't matter if I did or didn't." Taking one boot off, I threw it against the opposite wall.

"Wait." He rose from the floor. He bent to unlace and remove my remaining boot. Sitting on the edge of the bed, he sighed and let it drop to the floor.

"Sorry. Long day." I rubbed my eyes. My eyelids felt like tiny pieces of sandpaper.

"You look as if you might pass out at any moment. I think you need to sleep. We're not going anywhere tonight."

I nodded, but attempted to keep my eyes open. Regulus moved to the concrete floor to stretch out. After a moment, he decided to prop himself in a seated position against the wall.

"Oh, no," I stuttered. "You can't do that."

He raised one eyebrow. "I've slept in worse positions."

I moved over on the twin sized bed. "You can sleep up here." When he didn't move, I added, "I need to get home and that's not going to happen if you can't help because you didn't get any sleep."

Call me practical with a touch of masochism.

In silence, he nodded once and rose. I turned to face the wall with my body balanced on the edge of the thin mattress.

Regulus positioned himself on the remaining mattress space before exhaling aloud. "Thank you." His low voice rumbled close to my ear, tickling the hairs on the back of my neck.

"No problem." I tugged the rough blanket around me and hoped I'd be able to sleep.

I needed to count sheep jumping hay bales or ninjas carrying throwing stars or zombies scuffling after me. I needed something disgusting, mind-boggling and stressful. Maybe calculus.

I needed to quit thinking about how close he was to me.

"Relax." Regulus's voice was heavy and sounded on the edge of sleep.

He rolled to face the door and we were back-to-back. I listened to his slow, regular breathing and allowed my own breaths to match his.

Chapter Seventeen

Company

I moved a centimeter at a time away from Regulus's side. Not wanting to wake him, I gradually lifted the arm I'd thrown across his chest. His chest rose and fell rhythmically like the slow tick of a clock.

"I'm awake." His low voice startled me.

"Um...sorry. I, um, didn't mean to—"

"I've been awake for a while." He shifted to a sitting position. "I didn't want to wake you."

"Oh." Heat crawled up my neck to infuse my face. I awkwardly pushed my body away from him and teetered on the edge before getting my balance.

"You act like I'm diseased," he muttered and hopped from the bed.

"Nope. Tired of being crushed while I sleep." I searched for something intelligent or witty to say as I stared at the wall, refusing to meet his eyes, hoping he couldn't read my mind. When he acted hurt by my less-than-friendly attitude, my insides squeezed painfully in a vice grip. Would I ever get over him?

Not likely. But I could give a performance worthy of an Oscar.

Regulus had risen and looked out the glass door. "How in the—"

"What?" The alarm in his voice sent a nervous chill up my spine that delivered goose bumps as it went.

"Come here."

I met him at the door. He moved aside to give me a vantage point that allowed sight of the other cells.

Four cells down, Em stood in the corner of the door with her face pressed against the glass. She lifted her hand in a slight wave before it slid down the surface.

I put my hand on the glass as if I could touch hers.

"I assume they didn't come with you?" Regulus said.

"They?" I was unable to take my eyes from Em's.

"Austin's in there too. I saw him a second ago." Regulus crowded me while trying to look out. He placed his arm and face over my head to see better.

"How?"

He stepped back and looked down at me with a grimace, then shrugged. "Now we have the bigger problem of getting us out of here."

"What do She-ra and the others want from us?" I turned away from the glass to face him.

"I don't know. We thought we could seek refuge here."

Down the hall, Em had fogged up the glass door with her breathing. She began writing a message with backward letters appearing one at a time.

"UR house. watched U leave. tiny. cell phone," she printed across the glass. Regulus read the words aloud.

A door opened and stomping sounded from somewhere. Em quickly erased the words with her sleeve. She backed away from the door in a ninja move that made me blink.

I went to sit on the bed and Regulus followed. If Arizona had told my friends to come, I planned to do serious damage to him.

"Relax. If we look nervous, it gives them an edge." Regulus examined our rigid, side-by-side positions on the bed. I shifted to a reclining position with my back against the concrete wall.

Regulus reached over to take my foot and placed it in his lap. He proceeded to massage it.

Which was ludicrous.

And a little creepy if I didn't know that it wasn't the norm for us. I was taken aback but tried to steady my breathing at the unexpected move.

I wondered if this whole thing he had about doing something unexpected to divert attention was an IIA tactic. Maybe the IIA had classes titled 'Diversion by Impulsive and Unanticipated Behavior.' I stifled a nervous giggle at the errant thought.

I had my attention on Regulus's hand rubbing my toes when a knock on the door startled me.

Two men stood at the glass door. One unlocked it by waving his hand above the threshold. I made a mental note to see how he did that parlor trick. I grabbed my boots and hauled them on when the other man motioned that we should approach the door.

A short walk later, after we were granted a restroom stop, we followed our captors without any handcuffs or other restraints to a large room that resembled a meeting area. Twenty or more chairs circled a long table in the center of the room.

"So, what do you think they want now?" I fidgeted in the chair I'd chosen at the table end. No one else had arrived.

"We don't appear to be prisoners." He held up his wrists and waved them freely.

"It's not like they're torturing us, but—news bulletin coming in—we are prisoners."

"I know you think being locked up with me is torture." His grimace at me was self-deprecating and sad.

I felt the emotion stab in my chest and slice into my barely healed heart. I remembered to breathe a second later.

"I never said that. Sorry. Confinement, starvation, no bathroom. Those things put me in a very bad mood." Trying to hate you, I mentally added.

He nodded. "We should make demands if they plan on keeping us."

"I don't know about you, but I'm demanding to be let out."

"Maybe they can help us."

I eyed him skeptically. "They don't look like they're in the mood."

"It's called bargaining." His confident smile made me swallow hard. I hoped he hadn't heard my gulp.

"Where is Arizona?" I was suddenly aware that I'd expected he'd be with us.

"I doubt they'll question us together."

"Why not?

"Arizona and I would be a threat together."

"What about me?" I crossed my arms over my chest.

"They're not worried about you." He dismissed me to look around the room.

"What if they are underestimating me?"

"Oh, they are certainly underestimating you. You could literally kill someone with your incessant questioning." While he continued his study of our surroundings, he put his finger in front of his lips and emphasized with a negative shake of his head.

He was afraid they were listening. I reviewed what I'd already said. *Great.*

The one door to the room opened to admit the two guards who'd escorted us earlier. They stood on each side of the door as sentries while several more men and women entered afterward.

A woman wearing some sort of body armor sat at Regulus's right. That was interesting. The others sat in the chairs nearest us at the table. A young guy with a friendly, open face smiled at me. His tousled hair gave him a carefree look.

Tousled Hair Guy began the questions. "Identify Regulus B7V."

"You know who I am," Regulus said.

The young guy smiled brightly. "Yes. It's true. You know we must. No harm in confirmation."

Regulus held out his wrist in a bored manner to the woman at his side. She produced a wand that she passed over Regulus's wrist.

"Good. Thank you."

Regulus inclined his head. "May I ask your

identification? Or do you have one?"

"You may call me Corona," he said.

"Thank you for your hospitality, Corona," Regulus said.

My head whipped to the side to stare at him. I managed to keep my mouth from a Grand Canyon sized drop at his polite and formal phrasing.

"And your identification?" Corona looked at me expectantly.

"I think you know that she has none," Regulus said.

"Mia," I said. "Why—"

Regulus put both hands on the table, face up. It was an odd gesture. "It is nothing to concern you. We appreciate your hospitality, but we cannot stay. This girl is with me."

"Why is she with you? We need to understand her purpose." Corona leaned forward and placed both his hands up on the table.

"The girl is unimportant."

"Sitting right here. You could at least use my name," I mumbled.

Regulus glared at me.

Corona turned his attention to me. "Mia, I would like to hear your information."

All faces at the table except for Regulus's turned to me. I could feel that he was holding his breath.

"Um...well...I am here with Regulus. But we are leaving. I'm visiting."

Regulus closed his eyes.

He may have even been praying, but I didn't think he ever prayed. Maybe he had just started.

"That is extremely interesting to us." Corona took

his hands from the table and leaned back in his chair. "Would you like to take a walk with me?"

Regulus removed his hands from the table and I sensed eyes watching his movements.

"We would walk with you," Regulus said.

Corona gave him a tight smile. "You understand that I wanted to walk with her alone, did you not? Where is your trust?"

Corona stood and held out a hand. "Come with me. You have nothing to fear. Regulus B7V will be here when we return."

I looked from Corona to Regulus, not knowing quite what to say or do.

"I insist. I would like to show you our facilities. You could talk with me about the food you prefer."

I wondered if I looked hungry. Corona had chosen the right thing to say to me. The pink color he emitted like a shawl around his frame told me he was excited, but harmless. I'd have known if there was danger.

"Sure."

Regulus stood and the woman beside him shook her head. She held a silver disk the size of a playing card. Regulus immediately returned to his seat and rested his hands palm up on the table again.

I rose but didn't take Corona's hand. "I'll be right back. It's OK," I said to Regulus. The nervous vibes poured off his skin and I wanted to soothe him. Regulus's actions seemed so out of character.

"Ten minutes," Regulus said. "I want her back in ten minutes."

Corona eyed him steadily. "She will." He grinned at me. "Come, before Regulus starts the clock."

Out in the corridor, Corona led the way while talking. He never looked to make sure I stayed near his side.

"Is he usually this distrustful?" Corona's pace could only be described as a stroll. No time demand by Regulus would worry him.

"Yes, as a matter of habit."

"That must be a very uncomfortable habit," he said.

"Uncomfortable, but safe."

He glanced sideways and chuckled. "So it is." He halted at the intersection of hallways. "Here we have the sleeping quarters." Corona nodded to a left wing. Turning right, he added, "Let's go to food storage."

"You didn't actually bring me on a walk to show me around." I peered at him to see his reaction.

"You are very astute. But a walk through the mundane makes serious discussion less...intense."

"So, tell me what you want from us."

"Are you searching for something in this place? Cassie tells me that Arizona should not be here. That he is here without authorization. I believe the same of Regulus. You..." He took a minute to stop and look me in the eyes. "You are not supposed to be here."

I raised an eyebrow, not wanting to give away more information than necessary.

Corona reached out slowly and took my hand, flipping it face up. He rubbed his thumb over my wrist. "No chip."

"How did you know?"

"We scan all those who enter our home to be sure. Your scan didn't show identification."

"Hmm..." The room we'd entered boasted shelves

of silver packets.

"And now we are to the problem that needs answering."

"Which package to eat first?"

He laughed and handed me a package. A transparent film proved that the container held what appeared to be dried apples.

"Open it," he instructed. "I like your confidence, Mia. Who are you?"

"You go first. Who are you and why did you lock us up?"

"A precaution. Arizona has stayed with us before. He and Cassie..." He wrinkled his nose, making me think it was a distasteful subject.

"Are good friends?"

"Yes." Relief washed over his face.

Did I seem that delicate? Or was he?

"And so Cassie captures her former flames and locks them up." I raised one eyebrow and popped a dried apple into my watering mouth.

"No. I've ordered the accommodations for security measures."

"Mmm." I savored the apple.

Corona smiled. "You're not worried about my intentions, are you?" The statement came out loaded with implication.

I knew he read more into my trust than I wanted. Maybe he knew about my synesthesia.

"Should I be?" I glanced sidelong at him and admired his soothing cool blue aura.

He laughed, a soft, amused chuckle that tickled my ears and made me want to join him.

"It's been too serious around here. Your honesty

and trust is disarming." He handed me another bag of dried goodies. "We have to return. Cassie wanted you separated from Arizona. She assumed you were paired." He signaled with his head that I should follow him out of the food storage area. "After Regulus's reactions, I'd say she was mistaken. He's very protective you."

"Habit." I immediately regretted the slip. "We're not...um...paired." I'd stopped munching on the apples at the sour note my thoughts had taken. I noticed the surroundings. "We didn't come this way."

"It's a tour. Remember?" he answered.

"OK. Where now?"

"Surveillance." He picked up the pace to a near jog.

Turning another corner in the winding maze, he opened a door to a dark room and indicated that I enter.

One wall served as a screen with dozens of video scenes.

"Here we have the ability to watch people in every corner of the city." He swept his hand in a circle.

I twirled to see that the opposite wall boasted more video. "So this is above our heads?"

"Above our heads and extending in a five hundred-mile radius in prime locations."

"Oh." I studied video of a riot. "Where's that?"

"Close," he answered. "Mia, I think you deserve honesty."

"Right. When are you releasing us?"

He placed one hand over his mouth. "We are holding you to protect you. Cassie requested this. If we let you go, you may fall into unfortunate circumstances."

"Is that a threat?"

"Do you really not understand the danger you are facing by being here?"

I glared at him. I'd tried to be friendly, but I was getting tired of his hinting and questioning. "I know and trust Regulus and Arizona."

"Regulus and Arizona are now fugitives. There are directives to find them and bring them to the IIA. They are to be detained if found. Another agent, Carina, is supposedly traveling with them."

"Who?" I stopped myself from gaping. A tickling warning traveled up my spine to set off the red alert. The name was too coincidental. Too unusual. Too me.

"Regulus and—"

"No. The other name."

"Carina?"

He didn't realize that he'd said my middle name. Or that he was baiting me to see what I'd confide. "So, do you get many visitors?"

"Time to return. I told Regulus a few minutes and I'm a man of my words."

"There's something in this for you."

"Yes." His steps slowed as he thought.

"What?" I could hear the cognitive wheels grinding while he hesitated. We'd stopped walking and looked at each other, assessing. I watched him twist a thin bronze band of metal on his wrist.

"You're Carina." His voice was low and even.

"I imagine I am."

"You aren't chipped." He looked around and stepped closer.

I stepped back. It wasn't that I thought Corona would harm me. But he was in my personal space and that alone made me nervous. Arizona did it to me all the time, but I'd gotten accustomed to his familiar attitude.

"We'll talk more later. Regulus will be wondering where we are." Corona turned and resumed a clipped pace.

I struggled to keep up. The switch in topics had been on edge, nervous. What had happened in that moment?

"Wait. You don't want to know why I'm not chipped?"

He paused, looked around, swallowed with a deep gulp, then answered in a rush. "There are plenty around here who aren't chipped until they're caught. People like us, down here living our simple lives away from the eyes of the Makers. The problem is that you are wanted as an agent *and* you are unchipped. That is unusual."

He turned and continued in a jog. "Later. We'll talk later."

He didn't even look to see if I had followed.

We turned another corner right and a left to stop at what I now considered my cell. I still held the food packages he'd given me.

"I apologize for this. It's necessary." Corona scanned his wrist across the entrance and the glass door opened. "Regulus," he said.

"Corona," answered Regulus. They did the head nod thing that only guys do. It seems that some gestures were universal, even in the Twilight Zone.

Chapter Eighteen

Regulus

Mia walked to the bed and sat beside him. "You OK?"

"Yes. OK." Regulus stared at the wall and gathered comfort from the fact that she'd sat so close to him. He'd wondered if she'd ever feel relaxed and let her guard down.

She scooted back until she sat reclining against the wall. Leaning her head to the side, she said, "That was different from what I expected."

"What did he say to you?" He needed to know everything. There was a reason he'd been told to stay behind. Corona could have told her anything and he suspected he wouldn't be portrayed in a good way.

She offered the two bags she'd brought back. "Here." When he didn't take one, she nudged him with her knee. "Go on. We have to eat."

Turning to her, he took the one with the dried

apples. "This is one of the things that draws me to you. You always look out for the people you care about."

"Huh?" She glanced at the bag he'd taken. "Not really. Just don't want you to starve before we can break out."

"Yes. I know." She acted scared that he might think she cared. But she did. No matter what she said. He'd never thought it important before, to have people who worried about his comfort. He'd always taken care of himself. He held the bag and watched her eat.

"You don't have to eat that. I'm not your mother."

"You'd make a good mother." Why had he said that? He was an idiot.

"Hmm..." She acted disinterested. "Not having kids. Ever."

"You cannot predict that."

"What about you?" She'd turned that back to him so quickly.

"The Makers decide that."

"Wow. Just wow." She shook her head and gave him a disgusted look, her nose wrinkled.

He frowned at her. His response had been automatic, trained, ingrained. "It's all I know."

"And why do they decide? Can't you just want to have children?"

"I'm sure they will ask me to donate sperm." Was that the right information to give? He knew the concept of this world was totally foreign to her. But the Makers created a strong, safe world for their people. He pushed his doubts to the back of his mind and rubbed his neck.

"Like into a sperm bank." She nodded. "I'm going to guess that the sperm bank ensures perfect specimens."

He twisted his head to look at her. "No one is perfect. Not yet."

"I met Caregiver. When Arizona and I came through the portal I was sick. Very sick. He took me to Caregiver."

"Did she know what to do?"

"I guess."

"I've never been sick."

"Lucky you." She pursed her lips and rolled her eyes. "There's nothing like the experience of having the flu or strep throat."

"Healthy me." He opened the bag and popped a dried apple into his mouth. He could feel her closing off, her arms crossed, her eyes focused on the wall.

"What did Corona say to you?" He tried hard to make the question light and conversational, but she had to know she couldn't avoid answering twice.

"That I'm in danger here and that you're wanted."

He hadn't expected her to say that. "That's true."

"The dangerous part or wanted part?"

"Both."

"He showed me the city on monitors. There's a room with a view from cameras everywhere. Did you know that?"

"Yes. But I am positive he showed you only the pictures he wants you to see."

She nodded. "Well, yeah. I guess. Do you know why he took me off alone?"

He shrugged and studied the apple slice he held. "I could guess. Or you could tell me to save time."

"I think he wanted to warn me. Or scare me."

He turned his head, rubbed the back of his neck, and nodded. "Yes. That would be true."

"How does he know my middle name is Carina?"

What did Corona know? "I don't know." He shrugged and didn't meet her eyes.

"You want me to answer the questions, but you don't play fair. No answers from you. Not one." Her voice had risen to a frustrated squeak.

"I really don't know how he knows."

"At least he talked to me."

"I talk to you."

"No, you don't. You answer questions with the least amount of information possible. You think it's not a lie if you omit things."

"Ask me the things you want to know." She wouldn't ask the important things. The things that had him thinking about her nonstop.

"Oh, you say that, but when I ask something really important..."

"Ask." He leaned his back against the wall and peered at her beneath his lashes.

"Anything?"

He nodded then turned his head in her direction.

"Why do you keep pushing me?" She looked at him with her head angled and brows lowered.

"Pushing? I don't understand."

"Why the kiss on Christmas Eve? It's like you're pushing me for some reaction."

"Wasn't that the reason for the mistletoe?"

"Yeah. OK. Next question. Why did you get me a Christmas present?"

"Again. That is something I am expected to do."

But that really wasn't true. In his world, he'd never given gifts. He wanted to see her smile, a smile that went up to her eyes.

"No. It's not."

"Yes, it—"

"How much do you remember?" She picked at the worn spot on one knee of her jeans. "About us."

He was afraid to answer. He didn't know the right answer. Usually the honest answer was the right one, but he couldn't risk getting this wrong. His relationship with her was the most confusing, frustrating experience he'd ever had.

"Why do you want to know?" Avoidance wasn't dishonest.

She shrugged like it didn't matter. "Curious."

"Very little." If he told her he remembered too much, she'd hate him for not telling her.

The lie hung like a curtain between them.

"That can't be true. I don't believe you."

"So, you are a truth-detector now?"

"Might be. I know when you aren't telling the truth," she said.

He sighed in defeat. "Occasionally, I get a feeling about something that is familiar and I associate it with you."

She leaned forward. "Go on."

"That is it. A feeling. It's nothing substantial. Nothing real."

"Feelings are real. I get feelings twenty-four seven. That's how I find portals. I'll bet you call that substantial, since it's something you need from me."

"That's not what I mean." He rubbed the back of his neck. "You are not an easy person."

"Humph." She ran fingers through her tangled hair. "Explain it to me."

"If you ask me about the time we watched a movie together, I won't remember. If you ask me to name your favorite food, I can't. If you want me to tell you about us, together, that memory isn't there. But sometimes..."

"Sometimes, what? Go on."

He rubbed his palms over his face. "A song or a food or place will make me happy and I connect it to you. I see your face. I see you smiling."

"And that doesn't that bother you?"

"No. Yes." He moaned. "The present is more important than the past."

"You're right." She shrugged. "It's our relationship now that matters. Or lack of one."

He made a low noise deep in his throat; it sounded like a hurt animal. "You are the most frustrating person I have ever met. I can't change the past. I can't change your mind about the IIA. I can't change the fact that you don't like me. I can only change the now."

"I've never said I don't like—"

He'd scooted over until his face was inches from hers. Her deer-in-the-headlights expression forced his predator heart to move closer.

Her big, brown eyes, rich and warm, spoke of innocence. A contradictory combination of trust and wariness that made him want to kiss her.

"This is now." He caressed her shoulders. When he intended to move back, to put space between them and block out the smell of her skin, she closed the distance.

It was all the invitation he needed. He touched her lips with his, slowly and hesitantly. A tasting that left him wanting more.

Her breathing quickened and she made a little sound that he wondered if he'd really heard.

His hands had fallen to rest gently on her hips. Her hands went around his neck and he moved closer.

Had it been like *this* before?

He knew this feeling. His mouth on hers was questioning, urging, relieving. Her soft skin, her warm smell, and her sweet mouth were exactly like he'd imagined for weeks.

Chapter Nineteen

Betrayal

A tapping at the wall broke the spell Regulus had woven. I opened my eyes, clearing my head in the process.

Regulus tilted his head. "I am tempted to ignore him."

I bit my bottom lip and blinked hard. "Maybe he's figured out a way to get out of here."

"I don't care right now."

I pushed him away and felt the cool air chill me when he sat up.

Moving to sit beside him, I stared up at the ceiling. Fantasy land of normal people and normal kissing—no, *hot* kissing—disappeared. Reality stepped forward.

"The IIA is looking for us. Corona used my middle name, but I'm not stupid. It has to be me. I don't have a chip. How do they know I'm here?"

He sighed. "Yes. It's you. The slang book Em gave me calls this a situation."

The *tick, thunk, thunk, tick* against the wall told me that Arizona was signaling in Morse code again.

Regulus listened, ear pressed to the wall, and I tried to wait patiently. I had so many questions. Questions that went beyond the cursory "How will I get home before my dad reports my disappearance to the police?"

"We have to escape. Is Corona going to turn us in?" I went to the glass door and squeezed myself into the corner. Em stood in the same position at her door. She lifted her hand in greeting. I saw her lips move and Austin's head moved into place above hers. I'd never seen her look so disheveled and tired.

"No. Corona isn't turning us in. If that were his intention, he would have done that already."

"How much trouble are you in with the IIA? Have you ever done this before?"

He came to stand at the edge of the door. "Done what?"

"Defy orders. Be a rebel. Do your own thing," I mumbled, staring at Austin and Em. They were arguing. Em could be passionate, but rarely got angry.

I watched her animated face flush red.

"Never." He spoke as though he was in a trance.

"Huh?"

"What's going on with them?" Regulus angled himself sideways for a better view. "Sweetheart."

He'd never used names like that with me. The word traveled over me like a caress. I took in a deep breath and my hands began to sweat.

"That's what Austin said to Emily," he muttered. "Actually, he cursed first and then called her that."

My face heated to the temperature of the sun at my assumption. Of course he hadn't been talking to me.

Em and Austin suddenly stopped their discussion as if they'd noticed they were a front-row spectator sport.

Austin moved out of the doorway and Em shook her head at me.

"What is going on?" I mouthed.

Em shook her head again and walked off.

* * *

We'd rationed the dried fruit and the additional bag of dried meat. A guard had escorted me for a restroom break earlier in the morning and I was grateful for small miracles. When I returned, a silver pitcher of ice water sat like a mirage in the corner of the cell.

"Do you do this every day?" I watched him complete another set of ten pushups.

"Mmm hmm." He didn't stop his routine, continuing on to sit-ups.

I'd been bored but this definitely had entertainment value. It would explain the abs I'd thought were some cruel stroke of good genetic hijinks.

He peered at me while continuing his exercise. If he thought I would look away, he couldn't be more wrong. I had nothing but time. I was out of my element in this world. Even if I figured out a way to escape, I had no clue what awaited me on the outside.

I had no phone, computer, television, or books. No wonder people in the old days had over a dozen kids.

I chided my imagination for wandering in that field of oh-don't-go-there.

"You never answered when I asked why the IIA is calling me by my middle name."

"Does it matter?"

"Oh, that's not evasive." I rolled my eyes. "Yes. It matters. No one calls me that. Why start now?"

"It is the name your mother agreed on giving you. The Makers requested it."

I shifted uncomfortably. "What do the Makers have to do with Nancy?"

He lifted one eyebrow and stopped in the middle of a sit-up, reclining on his elbows. "Why don't you call her 'mother'? You don't use your father's given name."

"I asked first."

He sighed then continued his sit-ups.

I groaned and rolled onto my back. "OK, OK. I don't call her mother because she didn't take care of me when I was a kid. I didn't know her. Satisfied?" I waited a beat. "Your turn."

"What do you know of your mother?"

"Nancy," I corrected. "Nothing really. Why do you think I'm asking you questions?"

"She was a research scientist when she was young."

"Yeah. Dad told me that he met her while she was taking soil samples on the mountain."

"Soil samples? Who told you that? She was a geneticist."

"Oh." Another dark secret that my father didn't know.

"She went to work for the IIA."

"As a geneticist?"

"No. As a portal finder. Did I not tell you these things? She was like you."

"Um...no. I'd remember this. And she was nothing like me." My heart was slamming in my chest.

"I only meant that she could sense things in the world that others could not." He stopped exercising.

Calm down. I began chewing on my thumbnail.

"Mia, stop. Mia."

The urgency in his voice startled me. "What?" I hadn't realized he'd moved from the floor and now sat on the bed.

He grabbed my wrist and brought my hand away from my mouth. "You're bleeding."

I stared at my tortured thumbnail instead of at him. "It's nothing but dead skin."

Instead of releasing my hand, he pressed it to his chest. "You're safe with me. You'll be home soon. You don't have to be afraid." His voice lulled with its musical quality.

I pulled my hand back.

"I'm not afraid. I'm mad. Do you know how mad I am?" I wanted to roar my frustration.

He shook his head, looking at me like I was the world's largest puzzle.

"I've been tricked my entire life into thinking that my mother left because she sucked. Because I sucked. Because our family was not enough for her and she wanted a different husband, or a different kid, or a different life. Well, who knew she was the great pretender. A liar. A thief who stole what every kid deserves. And now she's dead and I won't ever understand why she did this to us."

Sweat slicked my palms and my heartbeat thumped in my ears. I wanted to crawl into a tight ball, but he wouldn't let me.

Instead, he put his arms around me and held me.

"I can tell you the things you want to know. I have a file on Nancy Taylor, remember? I can tell you facts." His mouth was against my hair.

"Facts." I nodded. "You'll tell me everything in the file? You won't leave out anything?"

"Yes. But I also need to concentrate on leaving this place and getting you home. Getting Emily and Austin home."

"What about Bleeker?"

"He's probably far away from the Garden by now."

I pulled out of his arms. "We have to get him. If we're close, we can't give up. This place is the Garden?"

He brushed the hair out of my eyes and gave a tight smile. "Yes. This is the Garden. A place you are not authorized to visit. I should be here alone. Arizona was wrong to bring you." Regulus glanced up at the wall separating us from Arizona and frowned.

"He was worried about you. You're his family. Don't you know that? That's why he came."

"And what about you? Why did you come?"

I cleared my throat. My mind raced for something witty and noncommittal. Noncommittal in that it had nothing to do with him and everything to do with Bleeker. Noncommittal in that my heart wasn't a factor in my decision to risk my life. Noncommittal in that I couldn't stand the thought of anyone harming him.

Instead, I looked away, unable to meet his eyes.

"Back to my name. Why do they have a warrant out for Carina?" I asked.

"I almost forgot that question." He grimaced. "Mia Carina, Peter Antares. We're named for stars or systems. Our jailer Corona and the girl, Cassie, are too."

"And this is where I ask you to speak English. I don't have a clue what you are talking about." I frowned with an intensity I usually saved for linear algebra class.

"Sorry. We are named after the stars."

"Everybody has a star name here?"

"No. Only certain citizens have a star name."

"I'm not a citizen. And Pete isn't either."

"Nancy Taylor contracted with—"

A whooshing sound stopped Regulus from completing his sentence. The door to our cell had opened. Corona and Cassie stood with two guards at the entrance.

"We'd like to speak with you. Follow us to a more comfortable room," Cassie said to me. Her disapproving face said she didn't like me. After what Corona had said, I'd thought it was because she'd assumed I was with Arizona. Maybe not.

Regulus and I rose from the bed and began walking to the door.

"No. Only Mia Carina," Corona said.

"He comes with me. I'm not going without him." I edged closer to Regulus, hoping they wouldn't force me.

Corona and Cassie exchanged looks loaded with silent words. It reminded me of talking with Em and saying volumes with a glance at each other.

"Come." Corona beckoned.

"And Arizona. I want Arizona there, too." I thought I'd push for everything I could get.

I could almost see Cassie gritting her teeth. Corona smiled. Not an easy smile, but a recognition of the power play.

"Yes. Arizona may be present also. Any more demands?" Corona waved us to the door.

"No."

"Good. Let's go to the west wing," Corona said.

Several minutes later, we'd wound through a maze to end in the room I recognized from earlier. The minute I walked in the door, I heard Em's voice and wanted to cry from sheer joy. I hadn't asked for her, but she was there.

Regulus and I sat with Arizona and Em across from us. Austin was missing. Cassie and Corona each sat at opposite ends of our table.

Where was Austin?

Corona began the meeting by placing his palms up on the table in front of him. I watched Regulus and Arizona do the same. Finally, Cassie offered her hands in the same position.

Regulus looked at me and nodded to his hands. I shook my head in a tiny 'no' gesture, furrowed my eyebrows, aggravated at being asked to play along.

Arizona stared at me with pleading eyes. Cassie's

mouth tightened in a grim line. Her pleasant, golden mood turned brown as dead leaves. Everyone waited for me to join the ritual.

I took one look at Em's tired face and lay my hands, palm up on the table. I hoped it didn't mean that I surrendered to them in any way.

"We want your help," Corona said.

The surprise on my face must have been evident. Corona laughed and removed his hands from the table. I was relieved to put my hands in my lap.

"We also want information." Cassie looked at Regulus, refusing to make eye contact with me or Arizona.

"First, I need to know if Austin is OK," I said.

"He is," Corona said. Again the smile and the light, easy manner.

So much for an explanation. I couldn't imagine why Cassie was so uptight in contrast to Corona. I glanced over at Em's strained little smile.

"If Carina isn't chipped, how do they know she is here?" So, the niceties were over. I liked Corona and his straight attitude.

"Perhaps they are guessing," Regulus said. "How are you masking Arizona and me?"

"Interference is easy," Corona replied. "We aren't primitive here."

"Ah." Regulus nodded. "Good. I know you are compromising your people by having us here."

Corona nodded. "I think they know Mia Carina is in the Garden." He turned to ask me the next question. "Any recent injections? Surgeries? Medications?"

I shook my head.

"Perhaps her personal belongings have been tagged," Corona suggested.

"I don't think..." Regulus turned at me. "You didn't bring the cell phone with you." He stated it, unsure of my answer.

"I lost it after I got here." I was going to tell him that Arizona had thrown it in my bag.

"Yes. She is being monitored. I installed tracking in a weapon. The tracking was for me," Regulus said.

I stiffened at this little tidbit. My new cell phone monitored me. Regulus needed a lesson about boundaries.

Regulus appeared to be very unhappy. He turned to me. "We can talk about it later. I knew you were in danger. I'm sorry. I should have asked you."

Underneath the table, he placed a hand on my knee. I reached down and lightly squeezed his fingers.

Corona looked from Regulus to me. "Yes. Thank you for the explanation. This explains how the Makers know she is here."

"Our sources tell us that Mia Carina is a portal locator. We need to get a prisoner through a portal, away from the IIA and the Makers. We need your help. If you help us, we'll help you escape and take Mia Carina to safety."

"Where is this prisoner?" asked Arizona.

He'd been suspiciously quiet throughout the entire exchange. Since he was usually the talker in our group, I wondered what could be going through his head.

His engagement sparked Cassie's attention. "Magnum Opus," she said. "The prisoner, Vega, is in

Magnum Opus."

"And why is Vega being held?" I asked.

"The Makers have secrets within Magnum Opus. They think they've created a perfect human. We believe she should be freed." Cassie's chin rose and her eyes challenged me to judge.

"This is political?" I asked Corona.

Corona looked me, sadness creeping into his face. "Mia, our entire lives here are not about politics but about living with the right to exist and be happy. To be respected as individuals." He looked at Arizona. "She recently escaped and you returned her to the Makers."

Arizona's forehead creased. "The girl on the horse?"

"Yes," Corona said.

"Arizona told Cassie that you were already going to Magnum Opus." Corona leaned forward making eye contact with Regulus. "We have a way to enter but your way may be easier."

"I don't know that I have access. I intended to intercept someone on his way there," Regulus answered.

"Who is this someone?" Corona asked.

"He is called Eli Bleeker. He's wanted by the IIA," Regulus said. "And I think he was headed to Magnum Opus."

"We've seen the warning call and know of Eli," Cassie said.

Cassie was really quite pretty when she wasn't scowling. Her short, blue-black hair stuck up at odd angles over her head. A blue metal sword stuck through the cartilage of her upper ear. She looked dangerous and powerful. I hoped she didn't discover that Em had dated Arizona. It would put that ugly look right back on her face.

"We can help you find Eli and you will help us take Vega to safety," Corona said.

"We have more to lose. What do you risk? Nothing." A muscle ticked in Regulus's jaw.

"We'll send Cassie with you." Corona leaned in and put his palms face up on the table again. "You know it's the only way you will make it out. We know the coordinates within Magnum Opus. The portal location inside the complex changes."

I couldn't wait to ask questions about that place.

"When we leave you, we'll be tracked." Regulus stared at the wall over Em's head. For the first time, I noticed the appearance of a projected map.

"You won't be tracked while underground with us. We can get you to the entrance," Corona said. "If you agree, let us discuss logistics and plan. You and I."

"I am in agreement," Regulus said.

"Wait. I need to know why Austin isn't sitting here with us," I said.

"He is uncooperative and volatile." Cassie gave a delighted grin. "I like him."

"He's fine." Em punctuated her words with a sigh. "He tried to break out too many times, so they've cuffed him."

It surprised me when Regulus laughed.

"I can talk with him if you want him to stop." Regulus said when he'd stopped laughing. "He's an asset to us. We don't want him to trouble you."

"He cannot escape. We are worried about damage he may inflict upon himself," Corona said.

"Don't underestimate him," Regulus said.

"I'd like to talk with Em. We're not planning an escape or anything." When my request was met with silence, I added, "Please."

Corona nodded. "Later today. Cassie and I will meet with Regulus." He ignored Arizona's raised eyebrows.

"I should be there," Arizona said.

"You and Cassie argue too much." Corona scratched his chin in a thoughtful fashion.

"I should be there." Arizona wasn't backing down. He was also staring at Regulus for confirmation.

"He's right," Regulus said. "We need his creativity and impulsive nature."

I thought I saw Arizona cringe.

"I want to be there, too." The words galloped out of my mouth before I could corral them.

Heads turned to me. Cassie had a smile on her face. She hadn't seemed this happy since we'd arrived.

"I say she attends." Cassie looked from Corona to me and back.

"And I want Em and Austin there. If we are helping with this, we should all be there," I said.

Corona didn't answer immediately. We sat in silence and he appeared to think about my request.

"Yes." Corona stood and Cassie got to her feet as well.

"Cassie, please make certain that Mia Carina is allowed to meet with Emily in private. Take them to the bathing rooms where they may clean up," Corona said. "Regulus and Arizona will help with supplies. They need the exercise."

"I request that Austin be allowed to help. Physical activity will help tire him," Regulus said.

Corona nodded and led the way out with Regulus and Arizona following.

Em and I followed Cassie in a different direction. After a lengthy walk, we ended at a large pocket door. Cassie opened it and said, "You don't require a guard here. There's only one way in and one out. I'll be here when you finish." She made a motion with her hand to usher us inside.

"This is worse than the girl's locker room at school." I nosed through a stack of towels and toiletries in shelves lining one wall. "I'm showering after we talk." I sat on a bench. "Tell me how you got here."

"Tiny. He told us where to go. I don't know how he figured it out, but he said that he discovered the location while using Arizona's computer. Em paced like she was too nervous to sit.

"How did Tiny know we'd gone anywhere?"

"Austin and Tiny were with me when we got to your house and you were gone. We came because of your, well, your..."

"Say it, Em."

"Your mother. We wanted to be moral support."

I took a deep gulp of air. "I'm fine, Em. More than fine."

"Then, Tiny said he knew how to track you. And he did. He told us where to go and the rest was sort of blind luck."

I grimaced. "You call this lucky?"

"So, Tiny stayed behind to run interference with our parents in case we were gone longer than we thought. I actually thought you might be running away from home. I wasn't going to let you do it without talking to me and Austin."

"Are you crazy? I'm not running away. We were going after Regulus who was going after Bleeker. Alone. Without having to worry about you." My voice had risen and Em looked like she was torn between crying and decking me.

"I'm your best friend, and I am here to do what I have to do to keep you sane. Are you listening? You cannot push me away when times get tough. I'm here for you. Too bad if you don't like it." She'd balled her hands into fists.

I loved her fierce friendship.

"Calm down. No wonder you and Austin were fighting if you've been this tense. What was that about?"

"We were fighting about Arizona."

Chapter Twenty

Pete

Pete flicked his wrist skyward to examine the GPS readout on his military watch. He had permission to travel across dimensions, but it was not like Commander Evans had handed him a Rand McNally map. Checking the readout qualified as the mother-of-stupid things to do while in another dimension. His watch hadn't worked since he'd arrived.

Even a pencil drawing on a sticky note would be preferable to the verbal directions he'd been given. He had a few choice words he'd like to give the commander on his return.

Words he would probably keep to himself.

He waited at the entrance of the Godzilla-sized building exactly as he'd been instructed. The Vault. The jagged lines reminded him of a Jenga tower created by one drunk architect. What a pretentious name. Perfectly matching the small army of pretentious looking fellas who met him at the door.

"Peter Antares Taylor." A man eyed Pete like he'd study gum on the bottom of his shoe.

"I am." He answered as if it were a question instead of a statement.

"Follow me."

Pete glanced at the group escorting him. If he had doubted Mia's whereabouts before this moment, he didn't now. He hoped the IIA would listen to reason and negate a call for reinforcements.

He glanced at the cascading water walls as they walked to a sort of transport system. A tube, half tram and half Disney roller coaster, waited at the end of their walk. The group's leader pointed at a seat near the front.

A nice and comfortable ride, but one imprisoned seat with a safety bar. He'd rather walk, but he didn't know how far they were going. When the transport engaged, he blinked hard at the force. They were definitely going more than a couple of yards. He couldn't even see what they passed in the minutes from entry to stopping.

Adrenaline coursed through him like an electric charge. He imagined the worst. He took deep breaths and cleared his mind.

The IIA wouldn't kill her. At worst, they'd taken her to prove a point. Which was really stupid for interdimensional relations.

He exited the transport and walked at an equal pace with his escorts. At first glance, they'd looked alike. Now he saw the differences, slight differences.

The odd thing was the male escorts' similarity in physical build and height. He'd file that away for later.

They approached a doorway with a dim glow of lights around it. Maybe it was a sort of sensor or X-ray device.

"Welcome Peter Antares Taylor." A female smiled at him. Her black glossy hair fell in a curtain around her shoulders and softened her. "I am called Tiania.

He walked forward. "Thank you for agreeing to speak with me."

"Sit."

He sat across from her in the chair she'd indicated. The escorts moved from the room. One stayed inside the door and he knew the others were outside. Waiting.

Bravery and stupidity were two different things. Or maybe they were closer than he thought because her friendly smile mocked him.

"I'll get right to the reason for my visit," he said.

"Yes, do. This is highly unusual."

"My sister—"

"Mia Carina Taylor." She inserted the name crisply. As if she thought he'd need to be sure they were talking about the correct person.

"Yes." He controlled his emotions. Maybe she could read him. He wasn't able to read her, and it made him want to move closer.

A non-read on someone spelled trouble for him. The tension in his shoulder blades made a slow crawl up his neck.

"What can we help you with?" She folded both hands in her lap.

Pete looked at the man guarding the door and back to her. "I believe that you may know the whereabouts of my sister. If she is here," he said, "by mistake, I'd like to take her home."

The woman didn't answer.

He really wanted to take that overly helpful smile off her face. "If you'll let me leave with her, there'll be no harm done."

"There's some misunderstanding. Mia Carina Taylor is not in the Vault."

Would she stop with the whole name thing? It had to be an evasive answer. He knew in his gut that she was here. The fact that he'd been unable to locate Regulus and Arizona solidified his hunch.

"Do you have her location?" A direct question. Yes or no. He watched her reaction closely. She sat in the chair opposite him, three feet away and angled.

She crossed her legs and leaned forward. Her skirt, already several inches above the knee, rose two more inches north.

Oh yeah. The IIA put her in charge of this meeting on purpose. They were thinking his hormones would distract him, override his judgment.

And on some days, it would. But not now. She could be naked. Because he had superhuman self-control today. He didn't plan to lose Mia to these people.

"It is possible that we had a location." She uncrossed her legs. Again. Did the IIA believe his mind ran on one track? Yet, he *had* noticed. "And now?" He stared into her eyes, a robin's egg blue. Unusual. Had her eyes been that color when he'd entered? He couldn't remember.

"Her location is unknown," she said.

"But you had a possible location. Why possible?"

"The monitors detected someone without digital ID in the city. Our cameras confirmed that it was your sister. She accompanied two of our Enforcers. Enforcers here...unexpectedly. Your trip is wasted."

"How so?"

"Our agents had traveled into the city center when the location was lost."

"Lost?"

"Yes."

"Don't your agents have implanted chips?"

She sighed as if the interview had become boring. "Yes."

"How did you lose your agents?"

"It happens."

He resisted raising an eyebrow and calling her a body snatching liar. "When it happens, does the tracker appear again?"

"Of course."

"You won't mind if I wait until your agents are located again?"

"How long are you willing to wait?"

"As long as it takes."

She smiled, the light reflecting on her perfect teeth. "We are happy to host you. We'll assign living quarters to make your stay comfortable while you wait."

The phrase 'living quarters' slithered along his skin. He returned her smile, pushing past the warning of danger ahead. He didn't trust himself to do more than nod.

Pete stared at her eyes again. Blue eyes that had been brown when he'd entered the room. He was certain. He always noticed a woman's eyes.

"Follow me." She rose from the chair.

In the hallway, they returned to the transport. He'd figured out that the circular system allowed passengers to enter at the nearest point and be taken up, down, or to the opposite side of the Vault. The black glass sides of the transport gave him the uncanny feeling of being monitored.

A minute later, they stood in front of a doorway that he presumed to be his quarters.

"Am I authorized to leave my quarters?" He needed to know what they expected and even more important, what they wouldn't expect.

"You are not a prisoner here."

"Good. I'd like to know the parameters of my stay. Are there authorized areas for me?"

"Of course. I will accompany you to ensure you have a pleasant stay." She nodded at a man who'd shadowed them on the transport and stood a discreet ten feet in the background. "For your safety, Lan will be available outside your quarters. Inside your quarters, you will see a panel at the door that will allow you to communicate with me whenever necessary."

So much for saying he wasn't a prisoner.

"Thank you." He turned to the door which conveniently dissipated. Inside the room, he glanced around at the sparse setup. Worse than a guy's bachelor pad, the room had a bed, a small, separate bathroom, and a chair.

He sat in the chair and noticed a display on one wall. Tiania's face appeared on-screen, a pixel portrait of perfection. "Your meal choices are displayed to the right. Please state your order and I'll see that it's delivered."

He studied her blue eyes and the detail again disturbed him. Had the chameleon change occurred for a reason? He glanced at the choices.

"Steak with a side salad. Mashed potatoes. Rolls. Pecan pie," he said. They'd placed his favorite dishes on the menu selection. Again, disturbing.

"And a drink?" She locked eyes with him.

Could she see him or was it coincidence? He silently stood and walked across the room. Her eyes followed him. It was a dual display.

"Water is fine."

"Your meal will be delivered in five minutes."

"Thank you."

The image disappeared. The question was whether they still watched him. And that wasn't really a question.

Five minutes later, an older man stood at the door. Dressed in white, he looked different from the men who'd escorted him to Tiania. The difference wasn't in appearance but in the very essence of the man. Pete quickly realized why.

He felt tension from this man, emanating and twisting in a rush of texture. An interwoven blend of emotion and sweat. "May I come in?"

"Yes." Pete nodded. The man pushed a cart into the room. Domed serving dishes sat on the top of the cart and the man wheeled it next to the chair. It would serve as a table.

Pete meant to thank him, but the man walked out before he could say the words.

He sat in the chair and moved the cart in front of it. Five minutes but it didn't look like fast food. He cut into the steak. Perfect. Although he hadn't bothered to say he'd prefer medium well since he was so hungry he could eat it rare, it was perfect.

A tiny white triangle peeked out from the bottom of his steak. Paper. Maybe not so perfect.

Taking his knife, he lifted the steak to see a folded piece of white paper. He set the steak back onto his plate and lifted his eyes to the wall in front of him.

Had they seen him look under the meat?

He began cutting lightly into the beef, not bearing down with the knife. He placed the roll on his plate with the meat and potatoes. A larger roll would've been nice to cover his actions, but he only had the one. He forked a large scoop of potatoes and a bite of steak into his mouth.

If they looked too closely, a fine film of perspiration on his forehead would give him away.

He took a deep, calming breath.

A different attendant retrieved the cart. Pete waited a half hour and lay down on the bed. The lights dimmed automatically and he pulled the blanket to his face. The watch he'd worn through the dimensional portal had several handy functions. Upon pressing down, a low light shone onto the slip of paper he pulled from his mouth. Good. The paper had held together. He unfolded it several times and read.

Mia with Rebels. OZ made deal w/Rebels. Go to Magnum Opus to meet Mia. Leave at sunrise. I will kill surveillance. Got your back. Tiny

He relaxed for the first time since his arrival. Tiny had come through for him. The minute they'd left Arizona's dorm room that day, he'd known something incredible had happened. Tiny's eyes had glittered with excitement. Interest. Anticipation. The challenge of hacking into a whole new world had been too much to refuse.

And when Pete told Tiny that he was going after Mia, Tiny agreed to join the United States special ops force. Operation Zodiac needed a pro breaking into the impenetrable IIA's otherworld network. And while sitting underestimated and seemingly harmless at Arizona's computer, Tiny had stolen everything he had needed.

Chapter Twenty-One

A Plan

"Does he have a pair?" asked Cassie.

"Who?" We followed her quick pace through the maze.

"Austin," Cassie answered.

Em walked beside me in the narrow space and shot me an amused glance, one corner of her mouth twitching. "Pair of what?"

"No. No pair. He's a single," I answered, avoiding making eye contact with Em so I wouldn't laugh out loud. "Not dating anyone," I added for Em's benefit.

Em snorted and I had to smile. I don't know how she always made me feel better.

Cassie looked back sharply. "Is something wrong with him?"

"No, no. Nothing like that. We're both just being stupid."

She stopped for a moment. "You are very bright,

not stupid." Cassie was back to frowning. Fabulous. She continued power-walking.

"Austin is great." Em tried to salvage the camaraderie we'd had with Cassie.

We watched her back and waited for a response. I wondered how she and Arizona had been a 'pair.' They appeared to be polar opposites.

Cassie turned another corner, then stopped. "I can change the rooming partners if you like. Our citizens have private rooms, and there are no extras. We only have the three rooms you occupy at this time."

"Oh." I had not expected that. "That's OK...unless you want to switch." I looked at Em, waiting for confirmation.

"No. I'm fine." Em yawned. "Now that Austin isn't trying to break out like he's in Alcatraz, maybe I can get some sleep."

"Get some rest. I'll make sure they clean up before they return." Cassie waved to the hallway, not accompanying us the rest of the way. "We've turned off the locks."

At our hesitation, she added, "Go on. The outer doors are still very much locked. You can't leave."

"Thanks." I felt like an idiot for thanking our jailer.

When I entered my room, I noticed a bedroll and cushion had been added to the floor. I also saw a box of food and fresh water in the corner.

We'd obviously graduated to semi-guest status.

Taking a bag of an unidentifiable seed from the box, I munched on them until I was satisfied. I was clean, fed, and exhausted. The thought of crawling onto the bed and sleeping for several hours equated to winning the lottery.

"Need a nap?" Regulus asked.

I hadn't noticed he'd come into the room. "Yes." I stared at the bed. "For a hundred years."

"That would be a long one." He gave a warm, low laugh. "Go ahead. Rest. We have a meeting with the others this afternoon on strategy."

He waited for me to move. He gently gave me a nudge. I didn't argue. Regulus sat on the bedroll that had been placed on the floor. I lay down and let my heavy eyelids close, and a dream washed over me.

The sounds of distant water. The smells I associated with Regulus. The touch of a hand on my face. The slow and sure, musical beat of a heart.

I walked in a dark tunnel. Strings of whispering willow branches hung across the roof to swing in the breeze. Sunlight shone at the opposite end and a silhouetted figure waved me forward.

Dust motes drifted lazily in the beam of light.

The closer I came to the middle of the tunnel, the more I dreaded each step. Light flashed to illuminate the face of the person at my destination. The face of my dad. Darkness concealed his face. Light glittered and the face was Dr. Eli Bleeker. Darkness hid the face again. My feet stopped moving, not of my accord but by necessity.

Steel traps bit into my flesh as I pivoted to run back. Every movement cut the serrated teeth into my ankles deeper until the blood squirted out in unhindered arcs and my flesh burned.

"Come back," yelled Regulus. He stood behind me, tethered to a chain around his right ankle. I whimpered and pulled despite the excruciating pain, but I couldn't escape.

My stomach churned with an intensity that threatened to explode. I wanted to be violently ill. I needed to get out to help Regulus no matter the cost to my body. I feared I'd be too late.

A dark shadow crept across the entrance where Regulus begged me. His words confused me. "Run away," he said over and over, in a hoarse and broken voice.

I wouldn't leave him.

The traps enclosing my ankles sprang open and I ran to him.

"No," he yelled. "Don't."

A large mouth dripping vile black blood opened over the entrance of the tunnel. The poison dripped onto Regulus's hair the second before the gaping monster covered the entrance.

I crawled to the chain to find it empty.

Regulus was gone.

A hand grabbed my shoulder and I screamed.

"Mia. Mia. It's all right."

I opened my eyes and grabbed him close to me. "You're OK." My shaky breathing was muffled with my face buried in his chest.

"Shh," he murmured, smoothing my hair. "You were dreaming. I'm here."

"And you won't go doing anything stupid on your own. Not again."

"I never do anything stupid." He pulled back and looked me in the eyes. "Are you worried you won't get home? I told you that I'll make sure you do."

"We," I corrected. "We'll get home. All of us." My words came out with the unsteady quiver. He wasn't fooling me.

"That is the plan." He tilted my chin up gently. He looked down to see I'd grabbed his other hand in mine.

I loosened my death grip.

He smelled like heaven to me. A little earth, a little pine, a little cedar.

A little dangerous and infinitely good.

"Sorry about that. Got a little freaked. No big deal." I cleared my throat and blinked several times. "No need get all hero complex on me. This underground spook hotel gave me a nightmare." I scooted as far away as possible on the twin bed.

He narrowed his eyes at me and turned to stare at the door. "You don't have to be afraid of me."

"I'm not afraid of—" I didn't see him pivot or turn or close the inches between us. He was there when my mouth began to form the last word. His lips didn't touch mine immediately, he lingered at the edge of my mouth, giving me the chance to reject.

My eyes met his and I held my breath. He placed his forehead against mine and I closed my eyes against that moment I'd been wanting and dreading. The moment I'd give in and not fight his closeness. The moment that wasn't made of memories but of the present. The moment I admitted that I wasn't over him.

My lips pressed firmly to his—not in a shy, experimental touch—but in a challenge. His tongue teased my bottom lip and he pushed me down on the bed.

My heart raced and a fluttering in my stomach threatened to make me push the kiss deeper.

"Sorry to interrupt. We're meeting now." Cassie

actually did sound sorry. She stood leaning in the doorway with a knowing grin on her face. I wondered how long she'd been standing there.

My breathing hitched as I attempted to slide my emotional mask into place. He shouldn't know how much a little kiss affected me. If he knew, he'd break down that door to all my feelings and I'd be devastated. Again.

Taking in a mammoth lungful of air, I gave myself a mental shake. "Ready." I hopped from the bed as if nothing had happened and sprinted to the door.

I knew Regulus hadn't moved from the bed because Cassie waited, staring at him. I stood in the hallway, out of view and away from the glass door, doing a mental recitation of the reasons why I had to keep my distance.

Cassie sauntered ahead, glancing back curiously at our silent trek together behind her. I hadn't noticed her height until this moment. She acted so fierce and indomitable that I'd thought her my height or taller. In reality, she stood at maybe five feet three. She was also extremely slim through the waist and her biceps were cut like an athlete.

She waved us to the seats and took her place standing beside Corona. The guards were also present and a couple others who'd been there when we'd first found our way inside their underground complex.

Corona called the group to order. "We must plan carefully. We have an advantage we've never had before today. We have the chance to free someone who would be kept by the Makers—a woman living more as an experiment than as a human. We have the chance to show the Makers that we will be free of their manipulations and tyranny."

I looked at Regulus. He sat perfectly still, his face emotionless. Corona's speech had been impassioned and intended to incite, but he didn't react at all.

People in the group nodded their heads in agreement, muttering excitedly with a buzz only seen in mobs enraged by hate or energized by love.

"Why should we trust them?" One of the guards asked the question and eyes turned to us.

"The three—Arizona, Regulus, and Carina—are fugitives wanted for political crimes," answered Corona. "Mia Carina can locate the portal within Magnum Opus."

Political crimes? I hadn't realized that being here without authorization was that serious. My head swam with the fear that washed over me.

Regulus grabbed my hand and squeezed. Then he took my hand with his to the tabletop. He moved his to face palm up and I knew he expected the same from me.

I stopped breathing with all eyes on me as I slid both hands palm up on the table before me.

Arizona did the same and made eye contact with Em. She followed with her hands.

Austin sat with his arms free of shackles but crossed over his chest. After Em elbowed him, he rolled his eyes and joined the rest of us.

I looked at Austin sitting across from me and burning my skin with his dark glare. A tattoo cuff of barbed wire circled his right wrist. Dried blood reached from his tattoo to his fingertips. What had he done?

My intake of breath told him that I'd seen the blood on his hands. He winked to assure me that he wasn't hurt.

God bless Austin's rebel heart.

I shook my head a fraction, scared that he'd get himself killed before we could get out alive. The guy had DAREDEVIL written across him in screaming letters.

Our group began to chatter wildly and Corona quieted us. "Let us agree on a plan for Regulus to get into Magnum Opus."

"He can't go in. They'll know the minute his locator registers. We could cut the locator out of his wrist," said a beefy guard.

"We don't have the surgical requisites for that," Cassie said.

"No," I shook my head. "You guys are crazy if you think—"

"They are of no use to us," a woman I recognized from the first day underground called out.

Our voices rose again. Corona had lost control. Upturned palms had been removed from the tabletop and Regulus placed his hand on my knee and squeezed once before returning it to his lap.

"I'll go," Austin's voice was loud enough to be heard over the others.

"No," Em and I said in unison.

Austin ignored us. "Tell me what to do and I'll do it. No problem." He slung hair out from his eyes and winked at me.

"I appreciate Austin's honorable offer. But I will be the one going in. Not him," Regulus said.

I'd never wanted to slap someone so much in my

entire life. I wanted to scream and knock both their stubborn heads together. Sure, I wanted Bleeker and I did want to leave this place. I wanted everything back to normal in my life, but I wouldn't risk Regulus. I wouldn't. I brought one finger to my mouth and chewed on the cuticle.

"I can go with Austin and Cassie. I don't want Regulus and Arizona with us," I said.

"No." Regulus stood so quickly that he bumped my chair and several people came forward to restrain him.

The tiny hairs on my body stood on end when I realized how many weapons were pointed at Regulus. The room seemed to shrink and crowd in on me.

Sounds amplified and a wave of nausea swept over me so strongly that I swayed. The people in the room were tense and their fear, anger, and excitement thrummed in the air—pushing my senses to the brink. I put one hand against the table and the other on Regulus's arm.

"You can't leave here. You or Arizona. Your locator chips will give us away," I said in a low voice, pleading with him to listen.

Regulus's brow creased in tiny lines and he tried to refute what I said. I could practically see the internal battle as he tried to think of another way. He shook his head. "I won't let you risk your life."

He backed up quickly to extradite himself from my grip. His movement pressed the fallen chair against his legs and it screeched against the concrete floor. In my peripheral vision, I saw Cassie move toward him with her stunner.

"No," I said to her in the split second when I realized what she intended.

Regulus slumped forward, falling onto the table with a thump.

* * *

"You are insane!" I felt a little jealous of Cassie's confidence. Her impish grin floored me as she outlined the most outrageous plan for entering Magnum Opus. We'd spent three hours studying maps of the place and I still struggled to follow her descriptions. The corridors had names consisting of unfamiliar symbols and each room had a name that correlated with a star system.

"Toriga Core," I repeated. "Got it. And you are sure this is the right place?"

"She's sure." Austin hadn't stopped staring at her with a wicked grin since we began planning. I had to admit that it was refreshing. Rarely did I see Austin so smitten over a girl.

"What happens when we wave this thing over the scanner?" I asked.

"That's when we run to the portal with Vega. Are you sure you can find it?" Cassie squinted at me like she wanted to be reassured of my confidence.

"Yeah. No worries on that." I hoped that I sounded as convincing as she did.

"They will let the bots loose on us as soon as they realize that we've infiltrated the building." Cassie studied the wall with the maps displayed. "I'll make sure to get Vega to a checkpoint and I'll return here. But you won't have to help with that. I've done this dozens of times."

I raised my eyebrows at this revelation.

"What? You know that people enter your world for refuge. I think you call them Slips. It's what we do. We help fugitives escape to a safe place."

"Right," I answered. Cassie made it sound so normal. "Tell me about Vega."

"She is a Volo." Cassie tilted her head to the side. "A Volo. It means a wish. She is the Makers' wish for perfection. And because of her perfection, they intend to make more of her. She has traits beyond their expectations."

"More? As in more girls like her?" I pictured the face of the girl who'd fallen from the horse.

"Many more." Cassie grimaced. "It's the reason why Bleeker originally went to your world. To be a Keeper. He helped us smuggle the Volo to safety. Like Vega."

I froze. "Bleeker? You guys work with Dr. Bleeker?" My mind whirled like a carnival ride.

"Worked. Work*ed*." She laughed, a rich sound tickling my ears. "In the past. I should not laugh, but your face was so very funny. You looked like you discovered your mother was an Artificial or...um...something like that."

I still didn't laugh with her.

She coughed into her hand. "Maybe that was not a very funny thing to you. I apologize."

"Well, he's a very much a psycho killer now," I said.

She nodded. "Yes, we have heard this."

"What happened to him? If you think he was a good guy before, what happened?" I asked.

"I'm not sure. Maybe he will tell the IIA. Maybe not." Cassie began packing tools into a bag. "Maybe his family will know."

My head snapped up at that. "He doesn't have a family. Or I don't think he does." I remembered meeting him in his office at the university at the beginning of the fall. Dr. Eli Bleeker worked with high school students on science projects.

He did have photos of his children. He had mentioned his wife. It's how he'd won my trust in the first place. Later I'd thought it fake.

Where were they?

"Back to the plan, ladies. This seems too easy. Now tell us the things that could go wrong." Austin placed both hands on his hips and rocked on his heels, examining the maps.

"Plenty could go wrong. We will be lucky if only a few things do." Cassie answered with a wave of her hand. "The important thing is that we don't panic."

I nodded. "I need to know the plan for what happens to Em, Regulus, and Arizona after we go through. I can't leave Em here."

"Corona will take Em to a portal outside the city. He may take her as soon as we leave. It will be easier for the two of them to travel to the Outbounds," Cassie said.

"And Regulus and Arizona?" I tried to steady my voice.

"We give them Eli Bleeker. They'll return with him to the IIA." Cassie gave me serious eye contact. "You realize that your time with the IIA is at an end. They'll figure out that you helped us find the portal within Magnum Opus."

I nodded. "I know."

"Cassie." A voice came from a speaker. "The girl Em wishes to say good-bye to Carina. What do you want to do?"

"Take Em to my room. I'll bring Mia Carina," she answered.

I smiled at her. "Thanks. I do need to say good-bye."

Chapter Twenty-Two

Regulus

Regulus stood at the door, waiting for anyone to walk down the hall. He needed to move back to the room next door. Mia needed him. And he definitely needed her.

No one came.

"Cassie's a mean little thing. She really amped up the stun for you." Arizona sat against his bedroll. He resumed chewing the end of a pencil.

"She seems pretty gutsy to me. I mean, she's going with Mia and Austin." Em ran fingers through her hair, trying to untangle the crazy mess around her head. Her face was scrubbed free of makeup, and she looked her age for once.

Arizona sighed and leaned back against the wall. "They need her. It will be a miracle if they pull this off and don't get us all killed."

Em narrowed her eyes at Arizona. "You don't have

a lot of faith in your friends."

"You're right, Em. You aren't trained for this. I can depend on Regulus, but Mia doesn't know what she's doing. She is out there, wavering in her allegiance from one minute to the next. I'm never positive if she has my back or not. And Austin, he's...well...too impulsive." Arizona laughed. "I recognize him for what he is because we're alike in so many ways."

"What about me?" Em moved to stand beside Regulus at the doorway "Do you think I'm a stupid girl?"

"I never said you were stupid." Arizona shrugged. "You shouldn't have come."

"You are the absolute, most frustrating—" Em pursed her mouth. "You wouldn't know a good friend if she followed all the way to...to..." She looked around with a forlorn expression, eyes wide and downcast. "I don't know where we are."

Regulus closed his eyes in a long blink and let out a frustrated breath.

"Sorry," Em said. "I know you're worried."

"Worried? I am not worrying. I am trying to think and it's difficult when you two..." He waved at hand at both of them. "When you choose to have a lovers' quarrel."

They both stared at him. Neither said a word for several minutes.

"How many assignments did you have before coming to Whispering Woods?" Em stared at him, her head tilted to one side.

"One." He furrowed his brow, confused at the sudden shift in her thoughts. Why did she ask?

"Tell me about it," Em demanded.

"What do you want to know?" There had to be some reason she asked and she was distracting him. He turned back to watch through the door. He couldn't risk missing his chance to talk to someone. He needed to convince them to change their plans.

"Where was it and what did you do?" Em moved to stand beside him, obviously bothered by his lack of attention.

"A little town in Maine. We were sent to find a couple who had lived there for ten years but were recently discovered."

"And you found them?" Em moved her head into his line of vision.

"Yes. They were easy to locate."

"Then what? You brought them here?" Em pressed her head to the glass door.

"Yes." He exhaled. This girl loved to talk. When he'd been younger and training in the vault, he'd wished to spend time with females. The Vault Training facility housed males only. It wasn't a discriminatory practice. If there had been more females in his world, it may have been different. But females were sparse.

Mia didn't talk as much as Em. He enjoyed sitting in silence with Mia. And he didn't mind the things she talked about. What was Mia doing right now?

"And were they causing trouble in my world? Is that why you had to arrest them?" Em asked.

"No. They were unauthorized." He glanced back at Arizona and wished she would ask him these questions.

"Do you ever wonder if you ruined their lives? Did they have children? Did—"

"It's the way. I'm not to question my orders." His voice grew gruff from irritation. Surely she would stop this meaningless interrogation soon.

"But you're breaking the rules now. What happens to you and Arizona when you leave here?"

"We take Bleeker in and will get some level of reprimand."

"Why do the IIA still want Mia? Will they be the new Dr. Bleeker for her? Badgering her chance they get because she doesn't want to work for them?"

Arizona cleared his throat. "Em, come sit with me and leave Regulus alone."

"No. He needs to hear this. And you." She swiveled and glared at Arizona. "You are only worried about him. What about Mia? Do you ever worry about her? You're supposed to be her friend."

"Regulus and I have been a team for a long time."

"I get that. I know you guys would do anything for each other. Like I'd do anything for Mia."

Arizona nodded, relaxed his body, then closed his eyes. "After my mom died, I lived in foster homes. Strange families who didn't care about me. My father took me to the IIA—to the Vault—and my life changed," he explained. "I was thirteen and alone. And I had Regulus. But I don't expect you to understand."

Emily moved away from the door. "Hey, sorry. I didn't know."

"I'm not asking for your pity. I want you to know that Regulus is my family. I don't care whether you understand the IIA's motives or not. The IIA and Regulus have been my family when I had no one."

"Point taken." Emily put her hand on Arizona's leg.

"And the IIA and the Makers know what's best."

Emily removed her hand from Arizona's leg. "You are so brainwashed."

Regulus turned away from them. He was finished with this conversation that went in circles. He had no choice. *Did he?* He knocked harshly on the wall, hoping that Mia would answer. Was she in there?

Adrenaline barreled through his body at the thought of running out of time.

"Corona," he yelled. "Corona." He banged on the door. Kicked it once. Twice. Slammed his fist against it and smeared blood from his knuckles by placing his hand against it. He was losing control.

"You know that won't work." Emily placed a hand on his arm. "Come away from the door."

"I can't let her do this." He shrugged Em's arm away and leaned his forehead against the door.

"Corona will come back to let you and Arizona go after Bleeker. Beating up the door isn't going to help."

Emily had said the magic words. Corona would let them go after Bleeker. *Them.* Arizona could go after Bleeker and he would intercept Mia at Magnum Opus.

"Em, I need for you to do something." He considered giving her a charming Arizona-like smile but changed his mind. She'd do it because she trusted him. And because she knew it would be for Mia.

"Do you think you can get someone to open this door and let you say good-bye to Mia? I think they'll do that for you. When you talk to her, find out the plan and you can tell me." He walked forward and knelt beside her at the bed. He took her hands in his. "You cannot let Mia or anyone know you're doing this for me. Can you do that?"

"Piece of James Bond cake, I can." She leaned down and squeezed his hands. "No worries. I've got this."

Emily released his hands and went to the door. "Hel-lo," she yelled. "I need Cassie or Corona..." She waited ten seconds and began yelling again. Her bellows brought a surly looking guard to the door.

Chapter Twenty-Three

Mission Impossible

"Are you scared?" Em fidgeted in the chair.

Cassie had given us ten minutes to talk privately. It seemed out of character, but I thought she only did that for me. Maybe it was a chance for final farewells.

"No. I'm not. I want to get this over with. I've worked so hard at avoiding things and it's time for me to confront the problems. Do what has to be done. Does that sound crazy?"

"Not at all." Em put her hands on my shoulders. "But be careful. I need my friend."

"You be careful," I answered. "I'll be fine. And Austin will be fine. We're getting out of here alive and going back home."

"I'm glad you're so confident." She smiled. "It's good to see you this way."

"What do you mean?"

"It's like the way you act when you're racking up life points in Quest. All smiley and happy. I mean, I know this isn't a game...really not a game. But you make me think we'll make it."

"They've limited my options so I'm going to think of this like an escort mission. I make sure that our NPC Vega gets out. Everything up to this point has been level grinding."

Em grinned at my gaming references. "Tell me the strategy."

I explained what Cassie had shown me and Em listened, nodding periodically, and agreeing that it was crazy.

"They had this mapped out," she guessed. "It's like they've been waiting for you."

"No. I think they've been waiting for any lucky break. They're like us when we're playing Quest of Zion. Well, except that it's real. And a head shot will definitely mean game over. They see opportunity and they run in full force."

Cassie entered the room. "Sorry. Time's up. We have things to do."

* * *

Cassie placed a hand on my shoulder as we stood side-by-side looking at the maps.

I thought about Regulus almost kissing me.

Regulus telling me about Nancy's murder.

Regulus kissing me before he'd forgotten by way of the memory cleanse enforced by the IIA.

Regulus telling me the silly line from the Shakespeare play he'd been reading for his class.

Regulus telling me that I could sense portals and needed to be their gatekeeper. His gatekeeper.

"Mia? You're OK, right?" Austin's voice broke through my trance.

"Oh, yeah. Sure. Fine." I smiled at him.

"Let's rock and roll!" Austin shouted. He put his hand in the air and I halfheartedly gave him a high five.

Cassie turned to me. "Carina?" She hesitated for a beat. "I think Regulus and Arizona will be fine when they turn Bleeker over. They'll probably be reprimanded by the IIA. But the IIA will overlook their indiscretions."

I closed my eyes for a second. "But they'll be OK, right? You know that?"

Cassie nodded. Austin walked away from us and pretended to study a holographic map.

"Good," I said. "It's for the best."

"I would guess they'll be reassigned after this," Cassie said. Her voice held a soft tone.

"Uh-huh."

"I'm not saying you must, but I think it would be best for you to say good-bye. That scene at the table...well...Agents never act like that."

"Like that?"

"Lose control. Regulus and Arizona are trained to harness their emotions. I sometimes wonder if Arizona actually has emotions. Regulus, earlier today..." She waved at the table. "He didn't act like an Agent. He acted like a person with a lot of emotions he couldn't control."

I sighed a rattling, shaky sound that left my chest in a whoosh.

"I don't have to see him. We should go as soon as possible. He and I were...we were—"

She shook her head. "You don't need to tell me. I think you will regret it if you don't say good-bye to him."

I stared into her eyes. She knew how I felt.

"You're right. Can I talk to him?" I asked.

"Come with me." Cassie looked to Austin. "We'll be back quickly."

Austin shrugged. "Got nothing but time."

I followed her, wondering what I would say to him. My throat tightened from the effort of holding back tears. My steps were slow and unsteady. And then I stopped altogether.

She turned and frowned. "I don't want to take you if you will incite him."

"Huh?"

"He's going to try and stop you. Tell him good-bye but tell him it's for the best." Cassie gave me a look of pity. "If you let him see your emotions, I think you'll make it worse. Maybe this isn't good."

"No." I gulped in air. "Give me a second." I placed my hand on the wall and turned away from her. Taking several deep breaths and remembering all that was at stake, I pivoted. "Ready."

"Good. I knew you were stronger than that. You're like me. You do what has to be done. A broken heart or a weak mind won't save the ones you love." Cassie turned and gave me a sad smile. "You will be OK."

We rounded a corner and entered the hallway where we passed two rooms. At the third, I almost stumbled at seeing Em, Arizona, and Regulus sitting in silence.

Regulus jumped to his feet and hurriedly made his way to the glass door. Now unlocked, he opened it and stepped through, causing me to step back. Cassie walked to the far end of the hall to give us some privacy.

"Hey." I forced myself to look him in the eyes.

"Hi." Regulus took a step closer. "So you're not going." He gave me a relieved smile.

I shook my head. "No, I am."

His brows lowered. "I don't understand. I can get us out of here. They can't force you to do this."

"They aren't forcing me."

"You can't go out there without me. Corona was telling you the truth. It is too dangerous for you to be here."

I looked away. "So, it was OK for you to run off chasing Bleeker with me, but not OK for me to take care of this."

"Yes. Um...no." His eyes darted back and forth, searching for the right response. "I can protect you. You need me."

"Take Bleeker in and come back to Whispering Woods."

Regulus placed his hand on the back of his neck and stared at the floor with a tortured look that made my chest constrict.

I made up my mind in that moment. "I need to go back. You need to stay. It's the only way."

He shook his head in slow motion. "Why are you giving up?"

"I'm not giving up. I'm choosing to be strong. Choosing to do what's best for everyone. I have a choice. And I know you don't."

He wouldn't look at me and a bowling ball sized bullet of hurt slammed into my chest.

I signaled to Cassie. "I'm ready."

"Mia," Regulus said. "Wait."

I needed for him to hurry before I lost my nerve to leave him. "Hmm?" I asked, not trusting myself to say any more.

"You're the bravest person I know."

"Brave isn't always smart or easy but sometimes it's the right thing to be. No matter how crappy of an idea it may seem to you, I know this is right."

"I never said it was smart. The IIA will know that you've helped the rebels. You don't comprehend the risk you're taking. If you're caught in Magnum Opus—"

"What? They'll capture me? Kill me? So, they're pretty much on even ground with Bleeker. Killing to get what they want." My anger spilled out without my consent. I'd meant to say good-bye in a different way.

He lowered his head, not meeting my eyes. When he finally looked at me again, he seemed afraid. "No," he said hoarsely. "It's not their way. They'll perform a memory cleanse to wipe away the obstacles."

"Like I said...kill me. Aren't we made of those memories?" I cleared my throat. "Please take care of yourself. I'll miss you."

I turned to run before my vision blurred with hot tears.

* * *

We left for Magnum Opus. Since Cassie didn't

have a locator chip, we could travel undetected to the secret passage that would gain us entry. We'd been supplied with ropes and gadgets that I knew would be useless to me. But Austin was getting into the entire thing with his exclamation of 'wicked' every time Cassie handed him something.

The secret passage turned out to be a cave that backed up to Magnum Opus. Cassie told us that the cave was thirty-eight miles long. Fugitives who didn't know their way through the cave system could get lost and never find a way out. We'd be walking through the dark with Cassie for almost five miles before climbing to a secret door that popped into the bottom of a water purification room.

Cassie was to remove a section of the floor with one of her handy gadgets and we'd go from there.

Walking through the dark, devoid of sensory stimulation, I reveled in the quietness of it. We walked while hooked together by a cable, stumbling on the uneven terrain. The only negative aspect was the abundance of time alone with my thoughts, so I concentrated on listening to Austin and Cassie whisper together like they were on a first date.

"So, what do you do for fun when you're not breaking into an enemy camp?"

"That is what I do for fun," she answered.

"Favorite food?" Austin asked.

"I like dried better than canned. Sometimes the canned has an old, tinny taste to it."

"Brothers and sisters?"

"Maybe."

Their conversation continued through the miles and I don't think either one cared about the answers the other gave. The banter was merely intended for listening to the other's voice.

I was glad when we finally stopped. My boots weren't meant for hiking and my feet ached from lack of proper sole support. It was still pitch black but I could feel the buzz of something nearby.

"I think I feel the portal from here."

"Very good." Cassie's steady, pleased answer told me that she thought we'd make it with the prisoners to the portal.

A light shone. "Ready," Austin said.

"Five seconds," Cassie said.

Above our heads, with a silver object that resembled a pen, Cassie drew out a square shape while Austin held the light. I grabbed the square as it dropped. It weighed more than I'd estimated and I staggered to hold it aloft until I could place it quietly on the floor.

"Easy," Cassie said. "I'm going up first. I'll tap on the floor when it's safe to come up."

I gave her a thumbs-up.

It was still fairly dark, but Austin turned out the light that he held with a gadget that reminded me of a dime. "We got this," he said to me.

There was no way he could see me, but I nodded.

Tap. Tap. Tap.

"Up you go." I felt Austin's hands touch my waist. "Grab the sides of the opening and put your foot in my hands. I'll give you a boost."

I did as he instructed and pulled myself the rest of the way up. I puffed out a breath and tried to stifle the sound.

Banging my knees on the floor, I took a deep

breath and held my hand into the hole to help Austin.

"Move." He pulled himself up like it was no big deal.

I peered through the dim light where Cassie stood near a door at the other end of a gigantic room with her hands on her hips. Still grinning. Still cocky.

I shook my head and quickly made my way to her. She placed a thin translucent card over her palm and waved it at head height. The door slid open.

Austin and I followed her as she ran down empty corridors at full speed, stopping only at turns to look ahead before continuing. We struggled to keep up as she ran flights of steps like a football player running bleachers.

We'd studied the maps together, but I was already lost. I prayed we didn't get separated.

Cassie stopped and I nearly plowed into her. Austin grabbed my shirt to keep me from tumbling over. He rolled his eyes and smirked.

Cassie waved her hand over the doorway as she'd done before. The door disappeared and I saw the girl, Vega. We quickly entered, ready to grab the girl and run. She stood so still that I focused on her first. A white light illuminated her beautiful face. Her golden hair and ringlet curls cascaded down her shoulders. Her eyes were averted to the side of the room and that's when I noticed. Dr. Eli Bleeker stood to her right and pointed a silver cylinder at Austin's head. "Walk over here, Austin. It's very important that you do what I say."

"No, Austin." I moved an inch and Bleeker shook his head to stop me.

"Mia." He said my name with a fondness that alarmed me.

I gulped in air. I'd expected trouble. I'd expected the IIA or the Makers or a security system that would fry my brain as we'd entered Magnum Opus. I'd expected to have trouble finding Vega.

I hadn't expected to find Bleeker.

"Doctor," I said.

"Austin, don't move too fast. I don't want to melt your face by accident." A green haze of evil surrounded Bleeker's body, appearing like a layer of pond scum.

"Yes, we don't want that." I racked my brain for movies where the policeman talked to someone who'd taken hostages. I thought of the movie *Die Hard* but didn't think witty one-liners were going to help me with Bleeker.

"We have a problem," Bleeker said. "You know that I have nothing to lose by killing him." He cocked his head toward a noise like a dog listening to a barely discernible sound. "I think we need to hurry."

"What do you want Bleeker? You want me?" My desperate plea fell on deaf ears.

"Austin, you stand where Vega is. Vega," he said, "you dear, are free to go."

She stumbled forward, an uncertain look on her face. Cassie moved forward and grabbed Vega's forearm.

He'd confused me. What was he doing? My heartbeat thrummed in my ear. A rush of noise—not my heart—sounded too close.

"You want me. Not Austin. Me!" I screamed without control, thought, or planning. I ran forward, my feet too slow, my mind in mental quicksand, and pushed Bleeker away.

Bleeker's weapon fired in a stream of blinding light that shattered the glass windows behind him. Smoke filled the air. I could only see flames and glass.

Momentum shoved us both forward, out the building window, onto the ledge. My hands grasped for something, anything, but my body rolled, then slipped off the edge.

Only my fingers gripped the granite ledge and I looked down. Too far. I guessed that it might be four stories from the ground.

"Hang on." A voice yelled from the ground. *Pete?* That was impossible.

The ledge extended out from the building for several feet. If I could pull myself up...

A couple of feet away, Bleeker also hung by fingertips. We were both pulling up and trying to make it back to the surface.

My hands began to feel slick.

"Mia!" Austin's yell came from inside. "Where are you?"

I saw Austin's dark head move outside the window. Then, another dark head and Regulus was on the ledge.

He grabbed my wrists, dug his heels against the slick surface, scrambled to pull me up. He flung both our bodies as close to the building as possible when we saw Bleeker pull to his feet and jump inside the room.

"Don't let him get away." I screamed, shaking my head furiously. "Get. Him!"

Regulus dragged me into his arms and squeezed

me. He put his hands on both sides of my face and said, "Where's the portal? I won't leave until you're safe."

"Bleeker," I muttered.

"You," he answered. He pressed his mouth against mine in a hard kiss.

"Not now. Portal?" Austin yelled, doing a little hurry dance from foot to foot.

I looked up to see Pete standing in the doorway. It had been him.

"Everyone follow me." Pete didn't wait to see if we obeyed. He started running.

I pulled Regulus's hand.

"Good-bye, Mia." Regulus put two fingers to his lips and touched mine. "Go with your brother. No time to argue." He shoved me roughly. "Listen for once. If you care for me, do this. You cannot be caught."

"What about—"

He only said one word. "Bleeker."

* * *

I felt a burning sensation and smelled the acrid, frenzied excitement of people not far from us. Cassie's eyes went wide. "Run."

My heart thwacked against my ribs in rhythm with my feet pounding the hallways as I tried to calm myself.

Portal. Portal. Breathe. Portal.

"This way." Pete yelled over the sound of an alarm. "Follow me!"

"Carina, you take Vega." Cassie pleaded with her

eyes. She looked scared for the first time. Her eyes were huge and darted behind us and back to Austin. "I can stall them. I'll double back and lead the bots in a different direction."

"Bots?" I'd forgotten about that part. I remembered the tiny lights swarming us when Arizona, Regulus and I had been running through the underground garage.

I looked to see smoke filling the corridor. Had someone set the place on fire?

"Go faster, Pete. Cassie, stop!" My voice was hoarse from screaming.

Cassie had already turned to run the opposite way from us.

"Yes?" Vega said.

"Come on." I grabbed her hand. Vega's eyes darted to Cassie as she looked for confirmation.

"We're all getting out," yelled Pete. "No one stays."

We ran down one passageway after another, the buzzing and smells drawing me to the portal. I could feel the enemy at our heels. I fought the nausea that rolled from Vega as she doubted our escape. Her fear sent burning stings along my skin.

"There." Pete pointed to the last door of a corridor that went on too long. Austin reached the door but had no way to open it. He slammed the palm of his hand against the door. Gone was my carefree, wild friend—the daredevil.

"The card, Cassie, the card," I yelled, still running the last few feet.

She waved her hand over the threshold.

Nothing happened. The door didn't slide open.

I gasped as a heated tidal wave of fear rolled off

my companions. "No," I yelled. "No."

We couldn't run. A bot army of menacing lights appeared at the other end of the corridor.

Cassie's anger assaulted my senses. Vega's fear burned and tingled in my throat, threatening to close my air passages. Pete muttered curses under his breath.

"Tiny! Man, do something," screamed Pete.

I looked at Pete and my world stalled in its rotation during that second. Austin slamming his hand against the door. Cassie searching past the bots, thinking, strategizing, risking.

Why had Pete yelled Tiny's name? Was Tiny helping us somehow?

I had a flash of Tiny sitting at his computer in my own dimension, feeling that prickly sensation when you miss something out of the corner of your eye. I imagined his shabby bedroom in the run-down house he shared with his grandmother. A naked light bulb hung the ceiling, unornamented and utilitarian. An ancient handmade quilt provided the only spot of color in a room filled with the metal and plastic of Tiny's massive computer setup—a technological shrine.

Were the hairs standing on the back of his neck? Did he actually have any window into this world? Could he hear the thump of my heart?

Our door slid open.

My focus narrowed at the heart-stopping realization of alternate reality. We ran through the doorway only to discover the floor ended and our bottomless descent began.

Chapter Twenty-Four

Regulus

Regulus listened to Arizona without agreeing or disagreeing.

"They'll drop all allegations against us when we hand him over."

Regulus sensed that Arizona watched his every expression. A bound and sedated Dr. Eli Bleeker walked between them through the Garden area and to the outer perimeter of The Vault.

When Bleeker had exited the frenzy of Magnum Opus, Arizona had caught him as easily as catching a child.

Now, they had no choice but to take Bleeker in themselves. Their locator chips had been online since leaving underground. They were both monitored.

The Vault housed the IIA and the officials who would take over custody of Dr. Eli Bleeker, a man who'd used a population from Mia's world as a personal pool of lab rats.

"We'll be assigned another," Arizona said.

Regulus didn't want to hear about another.

"Mia's not the only portal finder." Arizona looked at the gates and sighed. "Sometimes teams dynamics are off, or a personality requires a new match."

"I'm not going in," Regulus said softly. Gently.

"I can't take him in alone. You're still recovering from that stun from Cassie. If she hadn't handed Bleeker to us, I'd likely have throttled her myself. Never trust a woman."

"I'm not going with you. I'm going back to Mia's world. Someone will help me."

"I'm not going back there without authorization. We can talk about this. Maybe we can persuade them that there's an error and Mia can be part of our team again," Arizona said.

"No. You're wrong. You should know this by now. You do know." He frowned and wondered why Arizona cared so little about losing Mia.

Arizona stared at Regulus. "We are both taking Bleeker in. Don't make me—"

"And you don't threaten me." Regulus spoke within inches of Arizona's face.

"You're not throwing your life away for her. I won't let you." Arizona yelled. "They won't let you come back. They don't forgive."

"You told them."

"What?" Arizona sighed. "Told them what?"

"You told them I was in love with Mia Carina. You did. I know there is no other way they could have known."

They stood for several moments in silence.

Arizona gave him a smile that tipped one corner of his lips. "You of all people should understand their power. Last fall, you were planning to leave with Mia. They would have disposed of you when they caught you. There's no way to hide." Arizona's voice was gruff, full of emotion.

"I was leaving with her?" Regulus said.

"Right. Giving up your entire life to be with a girl."

"Did she know?"

"I don't know. Probably. You'd asked me for help. For the name of someone who could remove your chip."

This area of the city bustled with activity and people walked around them, curiously staring at Bleeker in the shackles around his ankles. He'd stayed silent until that moment.

"I can remove your chip. Take me somewhere and I'll remove it in exchange for my freedom." Bleeker's voice was clinical, but persuasive. "I've performed many of these surgeries."

"How many died while you performed them?" Regulus asked.

Bleeker shrugged. "Not many. It's a risk, but I'll make sure you survive. The losses on Earth weren't important. I had other uses for their bodies if they didn't make it."

Arizona turned to look at Regulus, ignoring Bleeker. "I did it for you. You're my family. You were going to get yourself killed."

Regulus gave him a tight smile. "You've never loved anyone."

Arizona looked at the blue sky above the gates of

The Vault. "I'm not apologizing. I'd do it again. Relations with their kind will hurt others."

"Others like you?"

Arizona stayed silent. They continued taking slow steps to the entrance of the Vault.

"My error was that I thought it would change things," Arizona said without looking at him.

"It did change things."

"Not really. You two are still in the same place you were before."

"I don't understand." Why did he feel Arizona talked in riddles when he wanted him to speak plainly?

"You still love her." Arizona turned to him and gave him a smile. "And she still loves you. The memory cleanse didn't take, huh?"

Arizona had said 'still.' Regulus smiled at the thought.

He dropped Bleeker's arm and stopped walking with them. "You could come with me."

"That's not my life. You know that." Arizona hesitated for a moment, searching for the right words. "I wish you well. I'll do what I can to stall their search."

Regulus put his hands on Arizona's shoulders. "Until we meet again."

"Until we do," Arizona echoed.

Chapter Twenty-Five

Good-bye

I sat with the worst case of dry mouth I'd ever had.

"Austin. Austin? Cassie? Pete?" I struggled to remain calm. Vega stood brushing off her clothes, smiling brightly and I wondered if she had brain damage.

This didn't seem to be a laughing matter.

I turned my head toward a smacking sound to my right. I'd found Austin and Cassie. They were both on their knees ten feet away, kissing and not coming up for air.

I smiled for the first time in days.

Rising to my feet, I noticed Em's car on the dirt road not far from us.

Was it a mirage in the middle of the woods?

Austin and Cassie had stopped kissing and were looking at the car with me. His arm was slung carelessly over her shoulder and she looked questioningly from me to Austin.

"Trouble?" she asked.

"I don't know. I don't get it. What's her car doing out here?" I walked hesitantly toward the red Camry.

That's when Em stepped out of the car and began waving.

When we stood a few feet from Em, I finally found the nerve to speak. "Are you really you?"

"Who else would I be?"

"We left you. How did you get here before we did? I mean..." I couldn't stop sputtering.

"It's a portal thing. Someday, I'll explain it to you." She giggled.

I wiped embarrassing tears from my face. "I'm so glad everyone is OK."

"Me, too."

"So, you didn't see anyone besides Corona when you left?"

"Only Arizona and Regulus. They left to take Bleeker in and Corona helped me to get home."

Pete rubbed his hand over the top of my head. "Let's go, Sis. We need to get home and I also owe Tiny a big thanks. Dad's used to me disappearing, but he's probably been freaking out about you. There's only so much damage control I can do."

I groaned and felt like crying some more. Instead, I sniffed. "I can deal with it."

"It's only been overnight." Em said. "That time difference thing is a brain bender. I'm glad we didn't go back in time."

Pete gave Em's arm a little shove. "What a comedian you've grown into."

* * *

The memorial service for my mother was crowded. Every person in Whispering Woods seemed to have decided to attend. I'd answered tight lipped each time the elderly ladies told me how they prayed for our family and that time would heal.

I didn't tell them that I was attending the memorial service of a stranger. A person I'd never known. An enigma.

The only sadness I felt was for my dad. His face held a weariness I wanted to wipe away. My brother hid his feelings, and in that respect, we were so alike.

"You're staying tonight, right?" Dad said to Pete more as a statement than as a question. He'd been tense with Pete. I could feel the hurt in every question Dad asked. It's tough to repair the damage of leaving home without good-byes and contact.

"I'm staying through the end of the week."

"Good. I want to talk with you about working for me. I can offer you some programming jobs better than whatever you're working on in California." Dad's his mouth was set in a tight line.

Pete only nodded and looked straight ahead at the people approaching us to offer more condolences.

Em pulled me aside and I'd never been so grateful for some relief from strangers patting me on the back.

"You OK?" Em gave me a tight hug.

I nodded. "Tired of people. Just tired. I saw Austin earlier. What happened to Cassie?"

"She wasn't staying after she placed Vega in a safe

house. She said she does this traveling back and forth thing a lot. You'd think Whispering Woods was a dimensional airport."

"Poor Austin."

"I'm more worried about you. You miss Regulus, don't you?" She reached out to grab my hand and squeezed.

My throat tightened at the mention of his name. "Oh, I'm all right. It's for the best." I had to fake it. Fake it that I didn't feel like lying down and curling into a fetal position every day.

She looked at me with those knowing eyes. "Let's hang out together later when you can get away. OK?"

"Thanks, Em." I gave her a hug.

People brought food to our house after the service. Every person in Whispering Woods practiced the Southern tradition of bringing casseroles to a grieving family.

I wanted everyone to go home. We didn't need another green bean casserole.

"You know I can't stay, right?" Pete said. "I'm staying a couple of days and I'm leaving. The longer I stay, the harder it will be on Dad."

I nodded without answering.

He put his hand underneath my chin. "You could use some mascara or something. You look like death. OK, bad choice of words here. But you should eat something."

I gave him a shove. This was the brother I loved. The one who could tell me I looked like crap only to rile me.

"And you should mind your own business." I attempted a smile, but it was tough.

"I need to get some food in town. There are too many folks in our house today. Want to come?"

"I don't feel like it. I think I'll go up to my room and sleep."

"No can do. I can't guarantee when I'll see you next. I need to have someone watch me eat. You can advise me on the best milkshake flavor."

I rolled my eyes. "OK. I wouldn't want you to flounder over that momentous decision."

We drove to the local barbecue restaurant, a hole-in-the-wall that had five red, vinyl-covered booths for patrons. Pete still wore his black suit from the memorial service and I hadn't changed from my black dress.

"What's the next step for you?" Pete sat at the far side to face the door.

I shrugged. "Don't know."

"Sis. You need plans. You can't tell me that you don't want to start college and find some hottie to date."

"Don't pressure me."

"It's my job. Older brother job. I'm in charge of keeping surveillance of all hottie action in your future."

"I've grown up a lot since you left. You don't have to worry about me anymore."

He sighed. "Sorry. It's a lifetime commitment."

A girl with a pad of paper interrupted to take our order. She looked longingly at Pete, but he didn't even notice.

"I wanted to talk to you alone. About Mom." He removed a toothpick from the silver dispenser on our table and stuck it in his mouth.

"Talk."

"You shouldn't hate her."

"I don't. She's dead. Can't hate her now. Boy did that solve that issue."

"You know what I mean. Hate her memory."

"I said I don't. You have to love somebody first to hate them later. I didn't know her, so I don't hate her."

"She was memory wiped multiple times. It made her crazy." He stopped looking at me and stared at the toothpick he twirled between two fingers.

A throb started in my temple. The mention of a memory cleanse made me think of Regulus. I'd banned myself from thinking about him. Too bad I couldn't order a memory cleanse.

"Why did they do it to her? Why, Pete?"

"She wanted to protect us, maybe. I don't know. It's not like she left a diary. But the IIA didn't want Mom to love us. It complicated things for them."

"It's some heavy stuff to digest." I opened a packet of sugar, poured it on the table, moved it around in swirls. "Bad guys everywhere."

"Mom didn't start out as one either. There are things we'll never understand." Pete reached across and stopped my finger from making swirls in the loose sugar on the table.

"I don't have to solve the mystery. I want to move on with my life."

"It's also obvious that you should be working with me at OZ. I think I'm helping you make your choice." He smirked and nodded. "You should say it."

"What?"

"I want to follow in my older brother's footsteps

because he is a superhero."

I pressed my lips together to stop from laughing. "Holy ego, Batman. At least I'm not working for the IIA. Does that make you feel better?"

"You have commitment issues."

I decided it was time to change the subject. "When do you leave? Did your boss tell you to be back right away?"

"How can I leave when you keep getting into trouble?"

I gasped. "I do not, Pete Taylor."

"Yes," he said, shaking his head. "You do. And as the team leader in charge of this area of Operation Zodiac, I've requested they let you join someday."

"They let you be in charge of something? If I remember correctly, you can't even do laundry without turning my underwear pink." I thought about what he'd said. "I don't know."

He scratched his head thoughtfully. "Here's the problem. We both have this gift of synesthesia on steroids, so to speak. Right now, the IIA really wants it. So you need protection. Wherever you choose to go to college, you need to have someone looking out for you. And you have time to decide about what you want to do."

"I don't need protection." I'd been trying to stop biting my destroyed fingernails, so I creased a napkin into an origami box. I'd decided to be stronger, braver. Maybe even get a manicure someday. Or so Em said.

"I'd like for you to think about it. I've been hunting for new recruits. You might like the people I work with."

"Don't push me. I need time to make good decisions." That's when I realized that someone stood at the edge of the booth and behind me.

"Pete." The deep voice behind my head made me shake in my seat. The napkin trembled, so I placed it on the table and put my hands together in my lap.

"Do you mind if I sit?" Regulus stepped to the center edge of the booth where I could see him, since I'd remained frozen, not looking back and holding my breath.

I didn't answer but moved over. He slid into the plastic seat easily with his body as close to mine as possible.

"Thank you," Regulus said.

I was stunned and afraid and nervous, a hundred emotions at once.

"I don't get it? How are you here?" I looked from him to Pete.

Pete stood and exited his side of the booth. "You can eat my burger. I think I'll get back to the house. Bring her home, all right?"

"Of course."

I watched Pete walk backward for a couple of steps, his gaze on my face. He raised his eyebrows, then smiled and nodded before turning to exit. The smile was infectious and I found myself grinning so hard my mouth hurt.

"Where's Arizona? I don't understand." I tilted my head and studied the origami napkin in my hand.

"He didn't come."

"Oh."

"If I went back, they would know the reason I disobeyed orders. Even with taking Bleeker in, they would erase my memory and reassign me. And the IIA still wants you. They can be very persuasive. I left the IIA." He leaned forward on his elbows and stilled my fingers that continued to crease the napkin.

"So, you can do that?"

"Normally, no. But it appears that they'd crossed over the line with some activities in their agreement with your government. I went to Pete, and he gave me the information for leverage. " He held up a hand to stop me. "Yes, this doesn't surprise you. I know."

"What does this mean for you?"

He took both my hands in his. "It means that I was part of a negotiation that worked in my favor."

His hands holding mine felt so right.

I raised one eyebrow. "And?"

"I've been offered a position here. With Operation Zodiac."

I didn't think it possible, but my grin widened. "Really?"

"I hope I can handle my first assignment."

"What is that?"

"Monitoring this area for my boss, but with an emphasis on watching out for his little sister. I hear she's obstinate and argumentative, but I think I've also heard that she's a hot girl. I should enjoy it."

"Wow...I...um..." I was unable to put words together into an intelligent sentence.

A whimpering sound came from behind Regulus.

"I almost forgot." He got out of his seat, walked to the door, and returned with a brown cardboard box.

"Another stunner?" I raised both brows and leaned forward.

The box moved on the table. Another whimper

escaped from inside it.

"Open it."

I lifted the lid and rose halfway in my seat to peer inside. Two thick paws pounced against the side of the box.

Warm brown eyes met mine. "A puppy!" I jumped from the seat to lift if from the box. I trembled with excitement that I hadn't felt in since I was a kid.

"Ma'am, you can't have that animal in here." The waitress frowned at us.

Regulus gave her a devilish grin. "Can you change our order to take-out? I wanted to give her this special present. It's my fault."

I lifted the puppy from the box to hold him to my chest. "He's a cairn terrier. Like Biscuit." My eyes filled with tears.

"I know he's not replacing Biscuit. He's only a little crumb."

"Crumb." I repeated.

I looked up at the waitress, who still watched us. She shook her head. "Oh, for heaven's sake. Put the puppy in the box and you can stay as long as you're the only customers."

"Thanks." I held the puppy at eye level and let him lick my nose. "She said you can stay, Crumb."

The background noises in the diner dimmed when I stared at Regulus. He'd left everything he knew. Would he be happy? No one could give us that answer.

He had the strength to choose a path right for his heart and his mind. And I was strong, too. Strong enough to take a risk.

The risk would be worth it.

I deposited the wiggling puppy back into the box that Regulus had placed on the floor beside me. "I don't know what to say. I'm speechless."

"That is amazing. I don't know that I have ever rendered you unable to talk. I only need to know one thing."

"What?"

"Do you want me to stay?" Regulus's expression grew serious.

"We have a problem if I haven't made my feelings for you very, very clear. I obviously suck at telling you. I think I should show you the answer." I leaned over the table and grabbed his jacket to pull his head to mine. My lips crushed against his perfect mouth, letting him feel all the emotions in my heart. The emotions I'd hidden away when I was a coward.

I melted into his kiss—a high voltage hazard—and gave an embarrassing moan.

He caressed my face and pulled back. "A message more powerful than words. I like a girl who takes action."

The End